More praise f‹

VINNIE GOT

'This is a short sharp shock
speech of disaffected London youth better than anyone else'
GQ

'Jaunty, sexy and original ... a rousingly good first novel.
Cameron writes with one hand wired to the mains'
LITERARY REVIEW

'Like some distant, downbeat relative of Anthony Burgess's A
Clockwork Orange, Jeremy Cameron's earthily gripping debut
thriller is a fast, funny trawl through the territory of London's
new outlaw underclass ... a masterly piece of storytelling'
FINANCIAL TIMES

IT WAS AN ACCIDENT ...

'The pleasure is intense ... Jeremy Cameron has an
unmatched ear for the shady melodies of London's streets'
TIME OUT

'Ingenious, his streetspeak sizzles with wit and invention ...
engaging, eventful and original'
LITERARY REVIEW

'A wonderful thriller ... an absolute cracker, the superb
narrative voice, North East London streetspeak, is so
convincingly done that it makes the residents of Albert Square
sound like Dick Van Dyke in Mary Poppins. The result is, as
Nicky might say, a result'
INDEPENDENT

Jeremy Cameron was a probation officer in Walthamstow for 20 years. Other titles in the Nicky Burkett crime series - *Vinnie Got Blown Away*, *It Was An Accident*, *Brown Bread In Wengen* and *Wider Than Walthamstow*. He is also the author of *Never Again*, his account of walking from Hook of Holland to Istanbul.

Hell on Hoe Street

JEREMY CAMERON

hoperoad : London

HopeRoad Publishing Ltd
P O Box 55544
Exhibition Road
London SW7 2DB

www.hoperoadpublishing.com
This edition published by HopeRoad 2016

A CIP catalogue for this book is available from the British Library

ISBN 978-1-908446-46-6

eISBN 978-1-908446-52-7

Printed and bound by
Lightning Source

Acknowledgements

Thanks to Nabila Khan (Alam) and all her family for making this book possible.

Thanks to Terry Oldham for the stories, for the reading and for donating himself.

A lot of thanks to Rosemarie Hudson and all at HopeRoad for reviving and re-publishing this series.

PART ONE

THERE

CHAPTER ONE

BLEEDING DESERT EVERYWHERE.

Train standing still, middle of the desert, taking a rest. Maybe it died. Maybe we were there permanent, got to settle, build an igloo.

'Train stop,' went the old geezer by me.

'True words mate,' I goes.

'Chapati,' went his missis.

They carried on feeding me up. Nothing else to be doing, get bored and feed up the foreigner. She gave over the chapati.

'Missis,' I turned round and said, 'appreciate your feelings don't get me wrong only you give me any more nosh and I might do us all a mischief you get my meaning?'

'Chai,' she went.

'Now you're talking.'

They got out the flask again. Tea never as hot as it was when they made it ten days ago only you never want it too hot when you got air about four thousand degrees coming in the window.

'Cheers lady.' She never spoke any English only we understood each other like we went out clubbing together. Except they never did a lot of clubbing up Pakistan how I heard it.

New geezer came in the door to our compartment. Fuck knows where he sprung out of. Seemed to reckon we were undercrowded in there, needed his company. Feller was creased like he lived under a camel.

He clocked me up and down same as an eye test. Then he gave it thinking. Then he made his announcement.

'English,' he went.

'Walthamstow mate no problem.'

'David Beckham,' he went.

'Yeah Becks,' I goes. 'Comes from Chingford innit?' I hated geezers from Chingford. Except David's dad Ted was all right as it goes.

'You David Beckham?' he goes.

'No mate. Hard telling us apart mind. Both got good-looking birds.'

They all gave me the eye test. Sure I was David.

'Inswinging free kick,' goes the creased geezer. Spoke five words of English and we just went through them. Seven when you count David Beckham. Nine when you count train and stop.

'West Ham got ten good as him,' I told him. They all looked puzzled. Some reason seemed they never heard of West Ham.

'Speak English bad,' he goes. Two more words.

'Don't you worry about it mate. My Urdu ain't none too bleedin' clever neither. No problem geezer eh?'

'No problem geezer eh?' He just learned some more. I ought to give out lessons.

Train started off again. We all clapped.

There I was, stuck on a chuffer half a day past the middle of nowhere. Bit of a surprise. Not what you expect Monday, wake up normal in E17, reckon on Wednesday you got desert all round.

Time for the introductions, spot of foreign relations after they gave me a ten course dinner.

'Nicky,' I went, sticking out my mitt.

'Pakora,' went the old biddy putting some grub in it.

'No no mate,' I went desperate. 'My name's Nicky. Got a gaff up Howard Road up Walthamstow. Mum lives up Priory Court. Went to school McEntee. One GCSE. Plus Art only that don't count.'

'You have wife?' went the new arrival. Kind of sudden.

'No I ain't,' I turned round and said. 'Never got one of them.'

Started a shock wave. Lot of chat all round, plenty muttering and gasping. Old lady burst into tears. 'No wife,' went the geezer.

'I got my bird,' I goes. 'Name of Noreen. That do?'

'Pakora,' went the old biddy again. 'Chai. Chapati.' She made signs with her mitts like fatten me up. 'Wife,' she goes.

Reckoned I'd try for staying thin.

All started Monday night. Put it down to Noreen cooking.

Last time Noreen cooked they got an eruption at Krakatoa. Bit like her cooking as it goes. This time the eruption was what she planned for my week ahead. All a bit of a shaker.

She belled me dinner time.

'All right Nicky?' she turned round and said. 'You just cleaning them toilets?'

'Stretched out by the gas fire with four birds and a Pernod,' I went. 'Now you mention it. Naked like.'

'Make me proud Nicky. Tell all my mates my man cleans the toilets. All of them wanting to meet you.'

'Yeah right.'

'Nicky I'm cooking tonight.'

'Noreen you want a trank? You got brain fever? Whip you up the quack?'

'And I'm bringing my friend home.'

'Now you're talking. Meaning you never wanting for your mate reckon your geezer does the cooking, innit?'

'Course it ain't, Nicky.'

'Yeah course it ain't. On the pope's bollocks.'

'She got a problem.'

'The pope?'

'Nicky shut it one moment. Now you get down the High Street please and you buy the following. You with me?'

I got ginger and lemon and sweet potatoes and red peppers for the soup and then a spiced bun to go with it. Keep her mate hot.

Two years back I came out of nick and my mates got me this gaff on Howard Rd. I managed all quite nice on my tod for a start off. They doshed the landlord the upfront then we got it sorted for Housing Benefit. Noreen came calling, only the fittest sexiest bit of stuff this side of Canvey Island. So I got a gaff for chilling, I got little Danny my boy visiting, I got no agg off the Old Bill. I got the sweetest tastiest chick in the borough two or three times a week. Life was what they call perfect.

Then Noreen stopped calling two or three times a week on account of she moved right in.

'Mens is better suited to cleaning toilets,' went Noreen. 'And anyway their smells is always worse than girls'. Innit Nicky?'

I drank my tea and watched her bits moving in that shirt. She was verocious was Noreen.

'So who this mate we got coming then?' I turned round and said. 'Queen of Sheba or what?'

'My friend Alia from work Nicky. She got a problem.'

'She a looker then this Alia? She a hot bird?'

'Nicky never you mind winding me up, you never get past the front porch with Alia. Muslim innit?'

'Oh Gawd. Never were ravers them Muslim birds. Never goers.'

'Exactly.'

'You know what you're doing on that soup Noreen? You want any advice?'

'Shut it Nicky.'

'So how she got a problem?'

'Tell you herself Nicky. Be here in a few minutes. Lives round Queen's Rd, we get the tube together.'

'Never turned round and told me you got the tube with some bird.'

'You never asked Nicky.'

Women.

'Know what? You want to put some garlic in that soup Noreen.'

'Shut it Nicky.'

Fair enough. Let her make her play.

'Now you just stir it Nicky while I get in the bath, all right?'

'Never come and watch you? Want your bits rubbed?'

'Just stir the soup Nicky. Rub my bits later.' She gave a little smirk and she was gone.

Then no sooner she got in the bath than the doorbell rang.

I went to the window. Generally we chucked the key down. This time I took one peek at what was stood standing on the ground and I went down for opening the door myself.

She was one fit bird Alia.

'Jesus,' I goes. 'You're one fit bird and that Alia.'

'You must be Nicky. I have heard such a lot about you from Noreen. Thank you for inviting me into your home. Is Noreen there? May I come in?'

They creased me up, Asian birds. Best fucking bodies in London. Politest gobs in the world. All passed about fourteen A-levels. You got as near them as Christmas after next. More likely I come off the dole than put it up an Asian bird.

Reading from the top, Alia got black black hair half length wavy. She got a boat race creamy and shapy. She got mince pies dark and beamy. She got a conk right short with a turn-up. She got teeth for chewing you up with. Down below she got all the bits in the right places. Figure like a weather forecaster. Waist like a wolf. Legs like lychees. She gave me the full scale ten o'clock itch.

'That you Alia?' goes Noreen down the stairs. 'Come on in. Take no notice of Nicky.'

'She hardly clocked my mush yet Noreen let alone took notice.'

'Yeah and a bit. I heard you mouthing off.'

'It doesn't matter Noreen,' went Alia behind me, 'you said he was a bit of a joker, you said he was a very nice boy really and I must not take him too serious.'

Eh?

'Don't let him hear that Alia or he get his head swelled.'

'Very nice boy Noreen?' I went.

'Don't remember Nicky. Maybe I did say that. Monday morning probably when I got a bad head.'

'After I poked you up Sunday?' I whispered through the door when we went up. She giggled.

'Come on in Alia.'

We went in and sat down. No point getting the rum out when you got Muslim visitors. I got the coconut milk down. It was foreign anyhow.

'This is a very nice place Noreen. Is it yours?'

'Matter of fact,' I turned round and said, 'gaff's mine. Noreen only pays the rent, know what I mean?'

'Oh I see.'

'Housing Benefit paid before only then Noreen reckoned she'd save the Council a bit of dosh, moved in.'

'I see.'

I dished up the coconut milk and brought out the coke without rum. Then Noreen went out and got the soup in. Nothing for afters. Asking too much for Noreen cooking two courses. Soup and bun and a few bits.

'Alia got a slight problem,' Noreen goes when we started on the soup. 'And she want you to go to Pakistan Nicky.'

I near as spat my soup all over our guest.

CHAPTER TWO

G EEZER BESIDE ME put his bonce on my shoulder.
Foreigners always were a bit too friendly. I bashed him
and he moved off. Put it on the geezer the other side and
started up snoring.

Lady with the chapatis got a scarf over her boat race. Hubbie
got his Judge Dread back against the board. Eight folk in the
compartment and only me and the lady not snoring, her on
account of she was a bird and me on account of I was awake.

We stopped. Middle of the night we were up some town,
hundreds on the platform getting on and selling tea and boiled
eggs and bracelets. My mate opposite took a butcher's and
groaned. No one else woke up.

Some time in the night I slept about five minutes. Dreamed
about Walthamstow. I was in our gaff on Howard Rd, popped
up Hoe St for a paper, came back and made a brew. Noreen
was ready for going off to her Uncle Bob, got a number doing
computers for British Airways up the West End. I could clock
breakfast TV then maybe go down the market and watch my
mates thieving out of BHS.

Only I was never in Walthamstow. I was further away from
Walthamstow than I reckoned you could get. Been through

the desert, still the middle of bleeding nowhere. Not a lot going down out there. Long way off to buy a paper. Get peckish and it was a fucking long walk for a take-away. Even an Indian take-away.

I was not one happy geezer.

'You see Nicky,' went Noreen again, 'Alia got this problem and she need to get it sorted right quick, you get my meaning?'

'Pakistan?' I went weak.

'Perhaps I had better explain,' Alia turned round and said.

'Perhaps it better you never go no further.'

'Nicky I already spoke for you,' Noreen goes. 'Seeing as how you're my man.'

'You already spoked for me?' I goes.

'You see Nicky,' Alia started off again, 'it is all about my brother Kamran.'

Long pause. I was smelling rats. Fact I was smelling so many rats you could start a rat farm.

'What your second name Alia?' I goes.

'Malik.'

Shit.

'So your bro, his name Kamran Malik?'

'Yes, that's my brother, Kamran Malik.'

'Fucking clever geezer? Bit of a footballer?'

'That's him.'

Noreen was sliding off in the kitchen, crafty little tart.

Long pause while I considered my options. None.

'Noreen?' I goes.

'Yes Nicky?' All sweet and innocent.

'You reckon by any possibility you were knowing how Alia's bro was Kamran Malik, went to McEntee with me and Vinnie and Jimmy and that?'

'Who me, Nicky?'

11

Say no fucking more. Noreen stitched me like a truss. Always knew I never could turn down any geezer I went to school with, point of respect. Except a couple went in the Old Bill was different. Noreen got me sorted all ways.

Shit and fuck.

'Carry on Alia,' I goes. I was stitched.

* * *

'Kamran went to Pakistan you see,' she turned round and said.

'Seems reasonable.'

'Two months ago. He went to see our family in Karachi and Lahore.'

'Fair enough.'

'And then we have never heard any more of him. He has disappeared.'

'Got some bird. No doubting it. Putting it up some Asian bird in some harem. Not likely he tell your mum and dad all the knockings. Keep it on the hush.'

'No Nicky.'

'No?'

'It is not a possibility. White families are like that. We Asian families are not like that. Kamran would not disappear.'

'Or put it up some bird?'

'Nicky ...' went Noreen warning.

'It is all right Noreen,' goes Alia. 'I understand what men are like, even my brother. But he could not do it in Pakistan. It is not possible.'

'They unnatural or what?'

'No, they are not unnatural Nicky. But they would not do it. And even if they wanted to they would not have any opportunity.'

12

'Get your meaning.' I reckoned there got to be a lot of birds panting for it out in Pakistan.

'So Noreen said, you being not very busy at the moment—'

'Unemployed,' goes Noreen.

'Very busy indeed,' I turned round and said.

'And also seeing that you very kindly got one or two people's problems sorted out for them before—'

'Full time job looking after Noreen, know what I mean? Very busy.'

'We wondered if you would consider coming out to Pakistan with me on Tuesday. To see if we can find Kamran, find out what has happened to him. If there has been …' she choked up, '… foul play.'

Tuesday. Today was Monday. How I reckoned it, Tuesday was tomorrow.

'So,' carries on Noreen, 'Alia got your visa in your passport today up their embassy.'

'Passport,' I went weak. 'In my drawer innit?'

Alia took it out her bag and showed me the visa.

Then she took some tabs out. 'And these being them malaria pills,' she goes. 'You start taking them with your supper, right?'

'You make sure you swallow them right down,' goes Noreen.

'And we have got you a ticket to go to Karachi tomorrow night at ten o'clock. I do hope you can make the trip Nicky. It would be so helpful. Noreen says you are just right for it and you know how these people's minds work.'

'These people?'

'Like the criminal mind Nicky. In case there are criminals.'

'You being one once,' goes Noreen threatening.

'PAKISTAN! I went. 'PAKISTAN! I DON'T KNOW FUCKING NOTHING ABOUT FUCKING PAKISTAN!'

13

'Why I'm coming with you,' goes Alia.

'DON'T EVEN SPEAKING THE FUCKING LAN-GUAGE!'

'Soon pick it up,' goes Noreen. 'Seeing as you speak French and that.'

Then I clocked it.

'What you turn round and say, Alia?'

'What about, Nicky?'

'About you coming … ?'

'Oh, that. Yes, we agreed, Noreen and me, that you would come with me. I am going anyway and you can be my travelling companion you see.'

'Oh …'

'Nicky …' went Noreen.

'Travelling companion?'

'Nicky …'

'I could not stay in the same place as you of course,' Alia turned round and said.

'No?'

'No. You see, Nicky, things are quite different in Pakistan. It would cause a very nasty business and people would think I was a prostitute. Of course I know you are very honourable and you would never try anything with me …'

'Course not,' I goes hasty.

'Never even cross your mind,' goes Noreen.

'But I shall not be far away and I will take you everywhere for the first week or so.'

'First week … ?' I goes feeble.

'Noreen says you will be perfectly all right after the first week or two. She says that whenever you go anywhere strange, like Jamaica or Tottenham, it takes you a little while to feel at home but then you settle down quite nicely. So I can take you

14

around and make all the introductions but then of course I must come back to work. Noreen says—'

'Catch your drift,' I went. 'Noreen spoked.'

'So we leave tomorrow night at ten o'clock from Heathrow,' she turned round and said. 'We should be at the airport by seven. This is very, very kind of you Nicky and all my family will respect and love you for it. We feel sure that you and I together will be able to find out what has happened to Kamran. Even if' – she went dark – 'even if it is something very bad.'

Then she came over and kissed me on the cheek. In front Noreen so I never took the oppo for stroking up her tits, bad career move. She smelled like a film star's bathroom.

'I got a snooker match Friday,' I goes weak.

'Ricky can play instead,' Noreen turned round and said. Ricky being her brother and that.

'He's playing already.'

'I can play then.'

'Birds not allowed. Spoils the atmosphere.'

'You just get up Pakistan Nicky, help Alia find her brother. Shouldn't be no trouble at all, probably his postcard got lost or he never learned to use the e-mail. We heard he landed. You just ask a few questions, find him out and then you be back by Christmas.'

Today was January.

CHAPTER THREE

NOREEN AND ME we got a system for doing the house work and sex. Least she got a system and I obeyed.

One thing I found out when Noreen moved in was how women went strange on you. You just marked them normal then they turned out not like geezers at all. One of their ways was how they were always wanting for doing something different.

Far as I was concerned you got a good habit you stopped in it no worries. So when Noreen reckoned she was sharing my gaff it all went sweet. She went off to work, I dossed round, spot of cleaning spot of cooking, she came home and we got a few spliffs and a Pernod and I put it up her. Sorted.

Then she reckoned she liked variety.

I reckoned variety came out of a box of chocolates. You wanted changes I favoured going out on a Friday for a few pints and a Sri Lankan across the road up Hoe St then a spot of nookie no problem. She meant maybe do it in the middle of the night or Saturday morning before I read the paper or even got a cup of rosie. Or down the marshes past the bushes where everyone came by and you got a cold bum. I never understood how you got your own gaff then you went outdoors for a touch of the other, seemed like it spoiled the whole point.

Women never were easy.

Then she started on the housework. Not the cooking on account of she never could be arsed, only housework she heard how it got to be shared for equality.

I learned early on about keeping my cell clean so I never got any problem round housework. Equality though was something I was never fussed over.

Noreen went how if I cleaned the bathroom Monday she did it Tuesday and when I got the sex on top Monday she got to be on top Tuesday.

Fair enough I goes. Start a rota no problem. So Wednesday me on top, Thursday her and so on. As it goes we always got a curry Thursdays so I got low on energy anyhow.

No! she reckoned then. Whole point is it ain't regular.

Me I was a regular geezer. Which was the whole problem with mens she reckoned.

So we started again at the start. One week she goes Monday I was on top and we got coffee instead of tea and we watched a video. Next week Monday her on top and we did it outside and we went up Tottenham for a Caribbean (Tottenham for fuck's sake) and we had a couple of lagers down the boozer even though it was Monday. Next Monday might be opposite or might be the same depending on her passion.

How Noreen felt was how the system went. But me I made it right tiring.

Next morning there I was doing a spot of shopping Noreen sent me out on before I went. Packet of washing powder, green type thing Noreen reckoned cleaned out the drains same time as your smalls. Half a yam, couple of dasheen, loaf of bread for my breakfast, half bottle vodka and an eighth of weed. Got a paper, on my way home for a cup when six little Asian bleeders jumped me, all about twelve.

Just turning in Howard Rd when they turned up on skates. Made a circle round me. Learned it in playschool.

'Nicky Burkett,' went one.

'Where?'

'You Nicky Burkett.'

'No mate. Some other geezer. Now you excuse me I got the kettle waiting.'

Little bleeder pulls out a blade.

'Do me a favour,' I turned round and said. 'Bit careful with that kiddo or you cut your dummy in half.'

'Teach you a lesson Nicky Burkett,' he goes. 'Keep your nose clean. Give you a good whacking.'

Maybe he never heard you don't give a whacking with a sticker. Give a shafting with a sticker, give a whacking with a rice flail. Anyhow this time of the morning you never give neither. Quarter to nine they were on their way to school, everyone else still in bed unless it was giro day.

'I go to school with your granddad?' I goes.

Then one of the little fuckers drops me, behind the knees special. And me still carrying the groceries.

'Could get vex here,' I warned them when they started kicking. Covered up with the shopping bag.

Then sudden there was a screech. Very very loud Urdu screech. Alia speaking her mind.

She came round that corner like bat out of hell. Never took prisoners no way at all.

Never lifted a mitt, all on the tongue. Gave them her views on them and on their mothers. All in Urdu they probably never understood any more than I did, only they got her gist. Legged it. No more heavy duty more like Boyzone.

'How you do that Alia?' I goes getting upwards. 'What you turn round and say to them?'

'I told them I knew all their families. Told them they face their dads tonight when they get home.'

'I was just started on sorting the little bastards,' I goes. 'When you interrupted.'

'Yes I could see that Nicky. Only it isn't very easy with that shopping, is it?'

'True words Alia, bit of a problem tell the truth. Anyhow why you ain't at work this time of day?'

'Late start today. I was just going down the tube station when I saw them following you. I think it might be my fault, Nicky. You see I think someone knows I have met you and wants to warn you off helping me and my family. I am sure of it in fact, that is why they were here.'

'Turned out the weight, eh?'

'Not really Nicky. I think the weight would be older. I think this might be just a little word that would not draw very much attention to them. I think it was assumed that you would beat them off but you would get the message about it.'

'Just starting on beating them off like I turned round and said Alia. Only the shopping you hear what I'm saying?'

'One thing is lucky Nicky, you will not be doing much shopping in Pakistan isn't it?'

Her smile gave me a knee trembler. Then she was off for work.

I went round Mum's for telling her I was away. That Kelly my babymother was there with Danny, how she took him to clock his granny once in a while. Strange how I used to reckon Kelly was the best poke this side of Princess Diana. Now I reckoned I rather have a pint of lager.

'All right Kelly?' I goes to her.

Then Danny came running up. 'All right Dad?' he goes jumping in my arms.

'All right Danny?' I hugs him. He gives me a smack in the gob, his way of showing affection.

'What you doing round here Nicky?' goes Mum like I was the loan shark. Shithead Henry her feller was at work, got a result there and we could get some peace. Sharon my sis was there and her kid, my niece or nephew I always forgot which. Sharon lived away now. Just visiting. Kelly and Danny visiting. It was quiet like the psycho ward.

'Came round for giving you news I'm away a few days.'

'Where you going Nicky? Pentonville? Scrubs?'

'What you mean a few days? You not paid your fines again or what?'

'Like one of them holidays.'

'Holidays?' goes Mum. 'I'll give you bleedin' holidays! And you on the frigging dole. Wait till I get on that scroungers' line they're always on about, grass you up good and proper my man don't you worry about that, time I finish they have the bleedin' Special Branch round and what they call it friggin' Vice Squad and Regional Crime Squad, throw away the key and you never see Christmas till January you hear what I'm saying!'

'Don't even claim Housing Benefit Mum, Noreen never stand for it. All light and creamy. Expenses paid.'

'Making a False Declaration, no two ways about that then, court on Monday afternoon, bang to rights and roll over.' We got some experience of the Social court on Mondays. Make the Mafia look like Bing Crosby.

'Where you going anyhow Nicky?' Sharon was a good'un, never let me down since we were kids.

'Popping out to Pakistan for a bit of work.'

That set Mum off hysterical. Sharon giggling. Kelly green with purple spots how she always was when I was around. All lasted about thirty minutes then their calmers kicked in.

20

'Drugs!' went Mum. 'Drugs! From Pakistan! I got to visit you up some nick in Singapore!' Mum watched a lot of telly, specialised in mothers clocking their kids coming to a sticky one round foreign parts. 'Death Row! Lethal injections! Russian Roulette!'

'I ain't going up Russia. And I ain't going after them drugs as it goes.'

'What you going there for then Nicky?' Sharon asked. 'That tourism?'

'Got a free ride. Going up Pakistan for seeing Kamran Malik.' Not so stupid as mentioning Alia when Kelly was around, even how we split up years off.

'Kamran Malik?' went Sharon. 'Went to school with us? Got a sister? Weren't he the clever geezer, bit of a footballer?'

'In one. Reckoned I go up that Karachi and Lahore, spend a bit of time with Kamran.'

They never knew what to turn round and say for this, if visiting some clever geezer was better or worse than drugs.

'Just don't you be asking for no help is all,' went Mum. Like I ever did. All I got when I needed an assist was her blubbing on visits whenever I got remand, nothing only serious aggravation gave me brain damage.

'What you want me bring you back from Pakistan Danny?'

'Kalashnikov Dad. One of them Kalashnikovs. With a silencer.'

'Not too sure they make them with a silencer mate. Still do my best.'

Then it clicked on with Mum.

'Free ride?' she goes. 'Free ride? And what you got to do in exchange for this free ride then eh? No such thing as a free ride Nicky innit?'

21

'Straight up. Freeman's catalogue. Like a holiday. All I got to do while I'm there is keep my hand in with a spot of robbing and hijacking …'

'You kept your hand in a few too many places you little bleeder.' Made Kelly blush brought back memories.

'Bring you back a gold tooth and a husband you want.'

'You get the back of my hand you don't watch it. Never too big for a bleeding smack.'

I went off for buying some teabags for the trip. I heard they never could make proper tea round those parts.

Noreen came home early on that flex time for packing my bag.

'Always take plenty underpants,' she goes. 'Never want to get caught out. Ten pairs.'

'Only wear one pair at a time Noreen,' I went. 'You reckon I start up import-export or what?'

'And three toothbrushes case you lose two. And soap and shampoo and scissors and cottonbuds and razor and shower gel and bath oil and skin cream …'

'Hang about Noreen,' I goes.

'Yes Nicky?'

'Cottonbuds? Them things in a tub? I ain't a bleeding bird Noreen. Geezers ain't got no use for cottonbuds.'

'And toothpaste and flannel and lip salve and deodorant and leg wax and talcum powder …'

I let her get on with it. Then when she went in the kitchen I emptied half of it out and hid it under the bed.

We got a cup of tea before we left. Sat down in the kitchen.

'Nicky,' she went.

'Oh Gawd,' I went. Knew what was coming.

'Miss you,' she went.

'Keen to get rid of me,' I told her. 'Never wait for packing me off with Alia.'

22

'Got to do it,' she turned round and said. 'Poor Alia she was so upset. And you being available for going with her. Miss you at nights though Nicky.' She started sniffing.

'Oh Gawd.'

'Get lonely weekends.'

'You want to do it now, Noreen? Before we go?'

She looked up her watch.

'We only got twenty minutes Nicky.'

'Do it twice in twenty minutes.'

She giggled and blushed. She thought about it maybe five seconds. Then we went sharp in the bedroom.

Noreen took me up Heathrow on the tube. Alia went up Heathrow in a few motors with the family. Mum and Dad, two sisters, three uncles, one aunt and fourteen cousins. Needed them all for carrying her luggage.

She took gifts for all the relatives up Pakistan. Made me take two of the cases like they were mine so she never paid so much excess. I dislocated an arm when I lifted one up.

Whole family clocked me up and down serious. I reckoned Mr and Mrs from when I was up McEntee. The rest, you never could mistake the Malik family. Whole lot looked healthy. Only problem with Kamran was he was always too fucking healthy. Made him stand out. He took some agg on account of it when he was young. Then it changed. First he started on the football. Then he did bodybuilding. Then he threw some kid under the 158 bus. Then the agg stopped.

So did the 158 as it goes. The kid got lucky.

They all wanted to know was I safe round their Alia or was I putting it up her twice a day already? Chance'd be a fine thing. Only way for catching a sniff of Alia's knickers was on the washing line.

23

'Hello Nicky how nice to see you again. Are you still playing football?'

'Not so often these days Mr Malik, bit old and that I reckon.'

'Ah, you must be, let me see, twenty-four or twenty-five now, isn't it?'

'All of that. Only not like your Kamran I never ate my greens, you hear what I'm saying? Misspent youth, too much of them prison and drugs, know what I mean?'

'We hear you have turned out very well,' goes Mrs. 'And we hear it is all down to that Noreen. We always thought you were a nice boy. Now it is very nice of you to go with Alia, you see someone must go with her and she cannot go alone and it is best if it is not …'

Meaning he was up some opium den or shagging some tart it was best they never sent family in.

'No problem Mrs Malik. Get him sorted right quick and back on the manor. No worries.'

'You are a good boy.'

'Nicky,' Noreen went. 'You better be a good boy.' Like a parrot.

Then they did the huggings. Alia near as kissed the whole passenger list. Noreen gave me a little peck on the chops, only when she was doing it she grabbed hold my bollocks in the bargain. Made me squeak.

'You be a good boy.'

After the huggings they did the weepings. Then they went off home and we went through and got up the duty free.

Alia started changing when we were up Heathrow. Then every hour she changed some more.

Meet her up Walthamstow she looked like any other normal bird. Heathrow she changed her jeans for the thin-type trousers. Get on the plane and she kept popping up the toilet. Every time she came back she was different. Skirt, top, jumper, shoes, probably her undies. Time we reached by Pakistan she got a shawl on and all the gear and she looked like she just stepped off the north-west frontier. Asian bird. Legit.

Me I looked like the same. Kind of cool.

'Nicky you like to lend a shalwar kameez off me?' Alia goes. 'They are just the same for boys as for girls you know. And they give you a very nice draught.'

'I got plenty of them whosits of my own,' I went. 'Don't need to borrow none. Only I save them for best. Manage in my Tommy Hilfiger thank you Alia.'

She made some noise kind of like a snicker. Ah well, birds.

Plane was full of passengers. Couple of dozen of them white and they all changed up Bahrain for somewhere. Rest were Asian grannys. Whole plane like full of grannys. Only a few kids and a dozen granddads, all the rest old biddies over about eighty. All going back for visiting their mums and dads maybe. Or it was some kind of granny festival up Karachi.

They gave us some nosh then they told us to go to sleep. Half the passengers were asleep before the nosh arrived.

They never flogged a lot of the old duty free on that flight. And me I stuck to the orange juice. Best not too conspicuous.

So I just got off snoozing nicely nicely, dreaming on the good old days thieving Teacher's out of Sainsbury's. Then what do I feel? Only Alia's hooter pressed hard against the top of my bonce. Her hot breath tickling round my fifth gear.

Now there was many a geezer never would pass up an oppo like that for a feel up an Asian bird. Me though I never even moved. On account of she woke up just when I was going to.

'Oh!' she cried.

'Pardon?' I goes like I just came out of a coma.

'Oh Nicky I am so sorry.'

'Mention it.'

'How embarrassing, I was pressing up against you.'

25

'Put up with it Alia.'

'My God,' she giggled. 'My face was right in your hair. I might have done something really awful.'

'Never grass you up Alia. Promise. Do what you like. Never let on to your Dad.'

'Oh and Noreen is my friend.'

'Mine too some of the time. Don't worry about it.'

Only then believe it she leant over the other way by the window and she went straight off sleeping again. So I did in the bargain. Afterwards it was like she never remembered a moment.

We changed planes up Bahrain. Plenty of sand. Couple of hours to wait so I bought six radios and half a ton of cashews. Asked about left luggage so I could pick them up on the way back. Turned out they never had a left luggage on account of bombs. And I was never coming back through Bahrain anyhow.

We got on another plane and I asked the stewardess she'd take them back home for me. She turned round and told me she was never as green as she was cabbage looking.

I never heard tell this was an old Arab saying. In the bargain she was giving me the glad eye. First off I reckoned this was it. I never met anyone got lucky with an Arab bird. Then it turned out she was never an Arab bird only dressed that way for a bit of work, name of Tina and she came from Leyton would you credit it. Reckoned she'd friend me up seeing as she heard the Walthamstow accent.

I never knew Walthamstow got an accent.

They gave us breakfast and more breakfast and elevenses and lunch. All happened in three hours, problems with the clocks. Then they reckoned it was Pakistan ahead.

We were there.

CHAPTER FOUR

W<small>E CAME IN</small> the airport me and Alia ready.
'Welcome to Pakistan,' went some geezer in the doorway.

'All right geezer?' I went polite.

'I respect your country.'

'You too mate. Ain't clocked a lot yet though.'

'I am qualified porter.'

'Glad to hear it. Always good get a qualification.' We carried on up immigration.

Then before we got there Alia started hissing like a snake. Came over all pale and sweating.

'Alia you all right girl?' I went.

'Piss on them all,' she turned round and said venomous. 'Damn them, bloody them, blast them, eff them!'

'Something bothering you mate? Pakistan too much for you? Need a trank? Couple of valium?'

'You do not understand what he said.'

'That geezer? Only welcomed me to Pakistan, fair enough.'

'Not him. That other man over there. In Urdu. He made a remark about us.'

'No problem some remark Alia. Reckoned you were a fit bird probably. Happen anywhere, body like you got.'

'He wanted to know what I was doing with a white man. And he did not say it nicely. He thinks I am cheap. And because I am a woman I am nothing and he can say what he wants.'

'No doubting you're a woman Alia, least not the way I sees it. Only he never got to diss you, fair enough. You want I fill him in or what?'

That started her off giggling, put her in a better mood straight off. 'Nicky you try to fill him in and he probably hit you with his sword or something. Damn man though. I hate them.'

'Got to stay cool, Alia. Pakistan ain't no different nowhere else. Some geezers ain't got no respect. Stay cool. Whack 'em when you got the advantage, know what I mean? No problem.'

'Nicky you will be finding that Pakistan is very different I think. It is not at all like Walthamstow.'

'Nah, Alia. You manage up Walthamstow you manage anywhere.'

We got through immigration, touch of the how's your father. Then we went off for picking up Alia's luggage.

In the collection area some geezer tapped me on the shoulder. Fact he felt my collar. Never knew anyone did that the last fifty years even Asian Old Bill.

He was in uniform. Not immigration uniform nor customs. He was Karachi Old Bill, wandered in there somehow off the street.

'You Nicholas Burkett,' he went.

'Nicky to my mates. Mr Burkett to you.'

'You come here.'

He beckoned me up some doorway. One of my rules always was, don't be going in no doorway with Old Bill. Whack you up or fit you up, either way stay out of doorways.

28

'No thanks,' I went. I stood there. Alia turned round and clocked me. I got witnesses.

He came over and leaned up my breathing area.

'You go home,' he went close.

'Pardon?'

'You go home. Not mix in business. Very dangerous. Dead.'

I gave him the big butcher's. He never moved. So I took out a pen for his shoulder number and wrote it on my mitt. Then he moved. Slipped away.

Alia came over quick.

'Nicky what was that?' she asked. 'You had a problem with the police? Did he speak English? They are very uneducated the police here you know. Very stupid.'

'Spoke enough,' I went. 'Catch his drift.'

Some fucker gave them the news on our trip already. Someone from back home. And some fucker out here wanted to know. Never liked us paddling in their pond. So they got the Bill out and they gave us the warning flag straight off. Mind your own manor.

Fuck 'em.

Through customs and we got met. First we got met by a hundred taxi drivers all wanting to do us a favour. Then we got met by a thousand of Alia's family.

Hard to believe she got any more family after what she left behind in England. I reckoned maybe she got three or four mums and dads, they never all came from one job lot. They could start their own country, Alialand.

They came in a fleet.

More of the hugging and kissing. Plenty of the birds were pieces of work only they never hugged or kissed me. Or shook hands. Geezers did all that and wished me the welcomes. Cool dudes in the bargain. Pleased to see me. Spoke English nearly like I did.

We flocked outside the airport.

It was Wednesday afternoon. Monday I still reckoned I'd be clocking *The Story Store* and the racing on Wednesday afternoon. I never heard of Alia. I never heard of her family. I heard of Pakistan like I heard of Whitney Houston.

Now I was standing in the sun so hot it reminded me of a motor we torched when we were kids. I wanted to stand further off. This was winter in Pakistan same as it was winter in Walthamstow. Likely it got hotter in summer.

I came over all faint.

Then we were driving into town in an old Saab. We were in Pakistan right and proper and there was no getting back on the plane.

CHAPTER FIVE

I ALWAYS RECKONED Lea Bridge Rd was as busy as they came. Step out in the rush hour and you moved in serious action. Stay breathing as far as Whipps Cross Hospital you needed a kosher attitude. Mean geezers and quality pollution. Least that was how I reckoned it before I got on Airport Rd, Karachi. Karachi made Walthamstow look like *Story Store.*

Mind they got a regular traffic system. All go like fuck.

On the junctions they got Old Bill. They got traffic lights only nobody paid them notice so they got the Bill in the bargain. Whistling away like a hundred referees except you argued and they shot you. Solve a few problems in the Premiership. Only trouble on Airport Rd was the action never happened up the junctions. It was all the bits in between where you got shafted.

They got lorries and pickups and scooters and pushbikes and they got horses and carts. Buses they filled up before they set off so any new passengers hung off the back. Ought to try that on the 48 up Lea Bridge Rd. They got four million motors, some of them BMWs and Mercs only most of them got born around the same time as my mum. They got taxis, most of them got four wheels some of them got four doors.

Then they got other things I got to clock several times before I credited them.

Rickshaws, Alia reckoned. Jesus.

Scooter engine on three wheels and a roof. Space for two small passengers. Hundreds of them buzzing like wasps, in and out the big traffic like close your mince pies and pray to Mecca. Had enough time on earth, kind of tired of the business, climb in a rickshaw and wait. Save the dosh on a funeral in the bargain, you got brown bread and cremated all in one hit.

Time we reached the city I was needing therapy.

'Nicky,' goes Alia in the motor, 'these are my cousin Rashid and my cousin Yasmin. They are my first cousins.'

'What are them others?'

'They are my first cousins too.'

Rashid and Yasmin were kind of intelligent looking. Bit plump and they seemed like they got a slight headache. Weary. Definite college type. I got introduced to them up the airport along with the rest of Pakistan so Alia did the business again personal. 'Very pleased to meet you,' we all went. Rashid turned round and shook me by the mitt. Then eventual he turned round and faced the front on account of he was the driver. Yasmin never touched me being a bird and might be getting the geezer lurgy. 'Very pleased to meet you indeed. We are very happy to welcome you to our country.'

Rashid and Yasmin gave the news in Urdu. Translated bits in English on my account. Everyone was getting married or university. Not a lot about getting pissed up or who was in the nick like most people. Kind of quiet lives they got.

While they yacked I kept my beadies on Death Race 3000 going down outside. Hit the floor every time some bus and two hundred passengers headed for coming in the windscreen. Somehow we got in the city.

Karachi got big buildings everywhere and noise and dust so you hardly clocked the other side the road. Everything brown except the new buildings not brown yet. Wide streets. Then we turned off down little streets for the houses. Like an estate only not like Priory Court where Mum lived, more like you never clocked the gaffs hidden behind the forestry. Big bushes and red flowers all over them, Hollywood touch. Then you got the message. Every gateway got geezers and every geezer got a shooter.

'This where them drug barons doss Rashid or what?' I goes.

'Drug barons, Nicky? Why do you ask?'

'Shooters Rashid. All the muscle got bleeding shooters. Got to be barons' manor innit?'

'I'm sorry, I do not understand your … your words. Alia?'

'He wants to know if drug dealers live in this area, Rashid, because all the security guards have got guns.'

'Oh .. .' Rashid pointed his viz outside the motor. 'Oh no, Nicky, this is good district. There are no drug dealers in this area, my goodness. Everybody has to have security guards here, you see.'

'Gotcha.'

'Everybody who lives in this district. Like us. Sometimes there are robbings and lootings and kidnappings and murders you see of the better-off families.'

'Yeah?'

'We have to employ some security you see. For protection.'

'Catch your drift Rashid.' Protection I knew about. 'Get your meaning. Villain city, say no more.'

'Here we are now. We have arrived at our house.'

Turned up another street on their estate, wide and quiet. Stopped by a white gate got the intercom. No need for using the Alexander though on account of a posse of geezers all geared up in brown were stood by the gate nodding and smiling at us. Happy to make our acquaintance it looked like. They opened the gate for us and we drove up.

'More family Alia?' I goes. 'Introduce us again?'

'Pardon Nicky?'

'Geezers in brown, more of the first cousins?'

'They are the servants Nicky.'

'Yeah?'

'There are servants here. Remember, if they are dressed in brown they are probably servants.'

'Course. Stands to reason.'

'You do not have to be introduced to the servants.'

'Fair enough.'

'But always be polite as a guest of course.'

'Course Alia. Treat them like my mum.'

'Better than your mum Nicky.'

'Oh. Yeah. Get your meaning.'

Then we got introduced to Alia's folks in white. Not servants. More like smooth rich bastards except they were Alia's. More of the Maliks. Uncle and aunt and granddad and about a dozen. Then they got kids. We moved into the front room for a bit of a pow-wow.

'Nicky we are very, very pleased to meet you,' goes Mrs.

'Welcome indeed to our country,' goes Mr.

'Pleasure's all mine, no problem.'

'This is your first time in our country?'

'First time, yeah. Still sorting out the sheep from the goats like.' Shit, was it sheep or goats Muslims never ate? I never wanted to give offence so I changed the subject. 'Take in a bit of culture, know what I mean, have a sniff round the old takeaways.'

'Er … yes, exactly. Do please be seated.'

'Then we came for putting the moves on old Kamran. Track him down, catch his ass and bring him back up Walthamstow, you hear what I'm saying?'

They parked me in a chair nearly sank into the southern hemisphere. Not so far from round there anyway so I heard.

Servants brought in the cashews. I wondered this was the meal so I took a pocketful. Polite like though. Then they brought out the gathia, always my favourite except it never was Noreen's on account of it caused serious wind problems. My mate Rameez reckoned it was the gram flour, well known for it. Made Noreen plenty vex.

Took my cue from the others. They grabbed it. Go for it, I reckoned. Never mind the fucking wind.

Then they brought fruit juices, mango and pineapple. Nice.

'I understand you went to school with Kamran, isn't it?'

'Yeah. Good mate of mine and Vinnie and Jimmy. Only problem he was such a bleeding sm ... so very clever. Passed them exams. Then I heard he was on West Ham's books in the bargain, couple of games in the reserves. Bit of a f ... bit of a goer was Kamran. Is Kamran. Charlie Big Potatoes innit?'

'He is not in Karachi to greet you I regret. He went to Lahore.'

'Lahore?' goes Alia.

'Lahore. He went to see the family there. On the other side.'

'Other side?' I turned round and said. How my mum always spoke when someone died off. Maybe they got ways up Pakistan I never knew about. 'He passed over?'

'He said he would be coming back the next week.' He got a result there then.

'Other side of the family Nicky,' goes Alia. 'Like mother's side and father's side.'

'Oh, hear what you're saying. No worries.'

'But we have heard no more from him and of course we became anxious.'

'Anxious.'

'But it was the other side and we did not want to cause offence.'

'Hear what you're saying. Family.'

'And then Alia's and Kamran's father and mother became anxious too. So we were very pleased when we heard that Alia would be coming out here to try to resolve the difficulty. With an escort.'

'Where I came in.'

'So we have booked you tickets to go to Lahore tonight.'

'Tonight?' goes Alia. 'On the plane?'

'Tonight's plane was regrettably full so we have had to book you on the train.'

'Oh my God,' went Alia.

'We knew you did not want to waste any time.'

'Oh my God,' went Alia again.

'But first of course we hope you will be able to take a small meal with us if you would be so kind.'

And I just gobbed half a pound of cashews and a bag of gathia.

We went in the dining room.

Walls of the front room were white. Walls of the dining room were white. On the floor they got a Persian carpet. On the table they got about a hundred dishes sitting ready.

Alia stood next by me.

'Alia,' I whispered. 'You never mentioned you was royalty. I only reckoned you lived on Queen's Rd, never knew you were the queen.'

'Nicky, this is life in Karachi for the better off,' she goes. 'There are many very poor people here as well.'

'Stands to reason innit? Some folk get rich, others got to be poor. Otherwise no one to get rich off, know what I mean?'

'Very philosophical Nicky.'

We parked our bums. Case a hundred dishes was never enough the servants brought a few more. They put a plate by me and another drink. They very near chewed my grub for me. I could get to liking being in Pakistan.

'Nicky, be careful with the food,' went Alia, maybe on account of she clocked me getting all excited. 'There is a limit to what you should eat of spicy food at first. It can do you a mischief you know.'

'Right Alia.'

'I think to begin with you should eat plenty of dal.'

I took her advice and ate plenty of that dal. And I leaned on the old spud and spinach a bit in the bargain. Gave the yoghurt a good whacking. Took in a plate or two of aubergines and a mixed veg. Couple of chapatis. Then on account of how I heard it was rude to turn down seconds in those parts I went round again.

Then they brought the fruit salad and coffee.

Coffee was crap. Rest of the meal was like putting it up a fit Asian bird in a five-star hotel with a couple of bottles champagne and a pipe of opium and a vibrating bed. Least I guessed it was. I never had any of them.

'Alia,' went her uncle in English.

'Yes uncle?'

'You understand you must be careful in Lahore.'

'Of course uncle.'

'They are very rough people in Lahore you know. Punjabis. It is not like Karachi.'

'No uncle.'

'If anything goes wrong, if you have any problems at all or there is any way we can help you must get in touch immediately, do you hear?'

'Yes uncle. Immediately.'

'We have connections.'

'Yes uncle. First we shall see the other side. We shall find out if Kamran is there or why he has not been in touch. Then if we need help to find him we shall call on you straight away.'

Uncle gave a little grunt.

The way I read it, he reckoned something was never pukka up Lahore. Something moody in the market. He was expecting the bad news breakfast any time now and he reckoned we might be bringing it. Or maybe he knew more than he was letting on.

I ate a few more cashews for afters.

Back in Parkhurst in the old days we got banquets.

Up Parkhurst you chilled out, everything cool. Before the crackdown you bought all the nosh you wanted. Got the folding in your private cash so the screws went up the supermarkets in Newport. Somerfield was cheapest. Then Saturday nights you had a party. So long as it stayed behind the door, nothing said. Alcohol out of potato peel and yeast, nicked off the kitchens. Maybe not what you give some new bird when you're after a Swiss roll but good enough for Saturday night on your tod. So we got pissed up Saturday nights and part of the process we got a banquet.

Course it was an accident me being in Parkhurst. Some geezer suffered a misunderstanding. Fact was he got off lightly. I totalled him so he never knew a thing, me I had to spend the next four years in various fucking nicks on a slaughter.

Parkhurst you cooked every night when you afforded it. Four cons in a food boat pooled their spends, curry seven nights a week. When it was your birthday though you saved up. I never could compete with the big boys but still when my birthday came round I got a seven-courser.

Leek and carrot soup

— . —

Melon

— . —

Cheese and biscuits

— . —

Veg

— . —

Potato curry

— . —

Lemon meringue or fruit (like a choice)

— . —

More cheese and biscuits

— . —

Hooch. Potato hooch or leek and carrot hooch
Dancing

I invited the screws for banqueting. Few of them showed
for the soup then they fucked off tactful before the drinking.
One woman screw I offered for the night, seeing most of the
wing reckoned they had her one time or another. Turned me
down though.

That was the last banquet I got. Only now up Pakistan I
looked like getting some more.

CHAPTER SIX

I GAVE IT brain.

How I reckoned it, Kamran went up Pakistan for visiting the relatives like they all did. Probably lining up some wife. Far as we knew he was never there for any agg at all.

Problem was some geezer up Walthamstow already clocked him going and never liked it. Or never liked us going after. We knew they heard up Walthamstow on account of I got the warning off the little kids.

So they marked his card before he even made his moves.

Then we reached by Karachi airport and what happened only Old Bill gave me the quiet word in the corner.

Alia's family reckoned all the Old Bill up Pakistan were bent and thick. Just like London. All the same this Old Bill up the airport never seemed like he got his wires crossed. More like carrying out an order. Maybe not off normal channels, probably going solo. Down the pocket of some warlord how I was thinking.

So the fuckers up Walthamstow and the fuckers up Pakistan were all knowing and planning something in advance. Something about Kamran.

Why?

Hard to credit Kamran was a drug smuggler. Such a goody two-shoes when we were up McEntee he never even bought chips with his dinner money. And still playing his football years later and training three times a week. Never appeared in court in his life. Then he got a number up some money firm round Liverpool St. Real work like on the cards and paid holidays.

Then I started the wondering. He worked up some money firm.

One thing I knew fuck all about was that money. Got no cause for knowing. Lettuce came by me it came in cash and it spent how it was meant to. Noreen took me up the Nationwide for paying in my giro was the first time I ever got an account. Till then it folded nicely and I still preferred it after. Cash cards were good for kiting about all.

So I hoped they never wanted Kamran for some money business, bit complicated for me. On the other hand if they wanted him for some cash, I was your man.

And you never could ignore the money bit. Or the cash bit. I gave it some more thinking. Have to see how the game panned out but maybe I was starting seeing light out at the end of the penalty area.

Not the easiest place for finding was their station up Karachi. Not the venue where the rich bastards went for their game of tennis, more somewhere you found when you were looking for a Chinese takeaway and a late-night spot of serious mugging.

They drove us down there half an hour before take-off. Getting in the station car park was never as easy as winning the lottery. Then a couple dozen geezers wanted to give us their assist. We fought a path out. Me, Alia and a few cousins, kind of a battering ram. We got into their station.

First off I reckoned it was a refugee camp like on the news, some war I never heard about. You stepped over families and tried not kicking their grannys in the mush. They were all over the station. Not a touch of ground. They never moved. No sign they ever caught a train. Sitting there patient waiting for something good or bad.

'All right geezer?' I went to some feller after I stepped on his mitt. 'Broke any bones in there?'

He gave me the cool stare like he never comped a single word I spoke him.

'Sorry and that,' I carried on. 'Bit tight round here. Got a train to catch. Hoping I get on it this week.'

'Inshallah,' he goes.

'About the size of it I reckon. You clocked that queue?'

He ate a bit more of his chapati.

Walthamstow Central always got geezers hanging round retailing travelcards and the *Big Issue* and a few items they never got a licence for. Only Walthamstow Central was a desert compared with Karachi station. And half the people there never did have a home to be homeless off.

Alia went pale. 'You all right girl?' I went. 'Alia?'

'Nicky,' she turned round and said. 'Even now I am sometimes shocked by Pakistan, it is true.'

'Hear what you're saying mate. Get the same feeling about Tottenham. Kind of basic.'

'Here is train,' goes a cousin.

Bit of excitement. Train pulled up by the platform. Four thousand people got up off the floor. Half of them went for getting on the train, other half taking the opportunity for a stretch.

Then geezers in uniform came out of all the doorways and drove them back.

'Not train,' goes the cousin.

'Not train,' I agrees.

'Not going to Lahore,' he turned round and said. 'Going for a refit is what they say. Myself I think maybe it got lost.'

42

'No problem. Wait for the next train, eh?'

What with them all standing up, this time we got some space on their platform before they all came back. We sat down. Alia and the cousins yacked in Urdu. I clocked round all the birds, only kind of careful case I brought down a fatwa. All the rest drank their tea and looked after their grannys and prayed. What you did. No video games.

Then another train came in. Turned up only half an hour after it was due to set off. It started a panic like West Ham just won at home.

Not only all the passengers went for that train, half the people not going anywhere went for it in the bargain. I reckoned it was likely for toppling over. The cousins turned round and said the night train was the quiet train. They set off for charging in there for my seat. Seemed to think it made no difference it being reserved, you still got to fight the Battle of Pollock's Crossing for it.

Back at the house earlier they explained it all, what happened on our train. Alia they booked on the ladies' sleeper. Fair enough, wouldn't mind getting in there myself. Only trouble was when they tried getting me in the gents' sleeper it was like fully booked. Very sorry they went only we got to book you in first class.

First class?

No problem geezer I went. No problem being first class with the nobs and rich bastards. Teach them some fucking manners, throw a fucking wobbly soon as they rattle their cage. Cousins looked at me kind of doubtful, still I never paid them any mind. Mix with anyone even first class.

So they went off and I waited on the platform till they called out my name. Leaning out the window along with everyone else seemed like they never all fitted inside. I wandered up the door then I clocked inside.

43

First class?

Cousins were throwing off the geezers and grannys all ways out of my reserved seat. Shouting and cackling and chucking all the baggage off after. No one was like complaining, all part of the trip. Spot embarrassing maybe how the grannys were kicked off for me, still you got to go with the flow.

When my seat was empty and I parked my bag on it and no one looked likely for arguing any more, I went back out on the platform. Alia was there too got her place sorted, looking kind of cool now.

'You all right in there Nicky?' she went. 'You comfortable, be able to sleep properly? They have reclining seats I know. It is not like a bunk but I hope you will be able to recline.'

'Plenty of reclining already. You sure that's first class Alia?'

'Yes I'm afraid that is first class Nicky. You should see second class.'

In our window you could clock a hundred passengers and four hundred bags and a few chickens. No goats. Enough food for a seven-year drought. Babies just born, probably a few more born before the other end. Geezers looked like they slice you up for forgetting a prayer in the morning. Granddads tell you the full story of the Hundred Years War. Bonus for being in first class.

Whistles kept going all round. No one took notice. Then sudden with no whistle everyone knew we were going.

'I shall see you in Lahore Nicky,' went Alia. 'Sleep well and have a good journey.'

'Yeah right.'

Which was where we all came in.

'Chapati,' went the lady.

'No mate,' I goes. 'No chapati. Handle a chai please. Plenty chai.'

'Chai,' she goes beaming, fishing out another flask from up the luggage rack.

Then we stopped up some station and some young geezer came on board with a pot and a dozen midgy cups. I bought chais all round, pay back some kind of respect.

We all did plenty of beaming then. Thick sweet chai for breakfast, we were ready for Lahore and any other fucking place.

CHAPTER SEVEN

I FELT LIKE I just got interviewed by four Old Bill in a quiet cell with no witnesses. I got a sore throat and cough and cold and brain fever and a touch of the old haemorrhoids. Come to Pakistan and catch a fucking cold, could do that at home. Air conditioning in their trains they stored their germs in, give them foreigners to eat when they got peckish.

Then I stepped out on the platform and that Alia was spitting blood.

'Eight hours late!' she was going. 'That train was eight hours late! We were supposed to get here this morning and now it is this afternoon!'

'Stay cool Alia,' I went. 'Hang chilled girl. This is the east. Always another day innit?' I waved the farewells to all the bodies off my compartment, going off with their bags and furniture. 'We get out of here and clock the manor, right? Few lagers, couple of spliffs and a spot of clubbing, know what I mean?'

'Oh, do shut up Nicky. There are times when you can be a real trial. You look terrible. We must get you to your hotel.'

Alia was off to the other side of the family. They were there for meeting us eight hours earlier only it looked like they got disappointed. She was staying with the family and I was in a

46

hotel, case we started a national scandal brought down the government.

When we stepped in the station we found out where the scandal was.

Alia went all fizzy-voiced again. Like road rage. Train rage. 'Damn damn damn,' she went. 'Damn and bother.' Strong words.

'Got another problem, doll?' I goes. 'Wrong time of the month or what?'

'Nicky Burkett! Do not talk to me like your white girls! Or black girls!'

'Oh yeah sorry Alia. Forgetting you was an Asian bird. Got to be you got a bad mark in your Maths exam innit? You just got a fax from home or what?'

'It was that man over there. Staring at me.'

'Yeah?'

'Staring so rudely at me. Making gestures. Because I am a woman and because I am with a white man I think.'

'No problem doll. Which geezer it was?'

'That man over there in the corner. The one without the moustache.'

Got to be a weirdo. Every other geezer in the station got a tash. This time I never waited for Alia's say so. Went over the geezer.

'Listen up John boy,' I goes.

He stared ahead like I was never there in his face.

'What you been lookin' at?' I carries on. 'You got a problem or what?'

He still never answered. Maybe he never understood English. I leaned up close in his range, poked him one in the kisser.

'Now you listen up geezer,' I turned round and said. Poked him another one. 'You keep on clocking up my bird with all that howsyourfuckinfather and I got to give you a fuckin' smack in the mush John, you get my meaning?'

47

He stared down the ground like he was the fucking innocent born yesterday.

'You hear what I'm saying Johnson?'

'No problem,' he goes. Spoke English obvious.

'You get my fuckin' meaning?'

'No problem.'

He got my meaning.

I went back to Alia. She was kind of quaking. 'Oh Nicky,' she went.

'No problem Alia. Me and old Hanif we understand each other now. No more of that anti-social behaviour. He got rehabilitated.'

'Nicky .. .'

'No need for all that Alia. We just get on with the business now, you hear what I'm saying?'

I reckoned she was too grateful for words. We carried on out the station.

'We going in one of them rickshaws Alia?'

'I was thinking of taking a taxi, Nicky. We will go in a rickshaw if you want to.'

'Same difference innit?'

'No, it is not quite the same at all actually. We will go in a rickshaw.' Then she started on giggling. 'We will see if you think it is like a taxi.'

Outside we got the choice, eighty rickshaws or a hundred taxis, all of them good rates like doing you a favour. Alia picked some quiet looking geezer. Minding his own business spitting huge red gobs in the gutter.

'Salaam mate,' I goes.

He tipped his bonce about a quarter inch. Definitely the quiet type. We got in the back. Then we got my bag in. Then we got Alia's two big cases, all the stuff she never left in

Karachi. The rickshaw got smaller. Then Alia seemed like she was saying a little prayer.

Driver went round the front with his crank for starting the engine. It started on the fourteenth go. Then he came back in still quiet like a dodo. Seemed to be reckoning whether he started or whether he just took a quiet kip instead.

Then he went off like a banshee.

Headed straight for the traffic. Where we got on the road there was never a gap so he reckoned on making his own. Bicycle on the left, motor on the right, two pedestrians standing in the middle and a truck bearing down on the lot of us. I took a gander at all of them and covered up my mince pies and waited for the smack.

Somehow next we were in the traffic. Never one to be put off his mission though, our mate drove under a bus. I put my bonce under his seat. Still no crunch. I looked up again and he was aiming between a donkey and a motor bike. Somehow they were both going straight towards us. Gap about an inch wide.

I clocked a funny wailing noise, turned round looking. It was me.

Alia still giggling along the seat. Birds always got their rocks off on geezers having some little problem.

Then we were over that main road and going down a side street, traffic only about ten wide down there. Almost straight off we took another turn then another. And up a long ramp and we were right in the Lahore Hotel.

Where they booked me. Kind of slick. Kind of a swish gaff.

We climbed out of the rickshaw, bit like undoing a ball of string where the string just got a heart murmur. Driver reckoned he'd wait outside doing a spot of spitting till he took Alia on. We went in the door and across the hall like a football pitch and up their desk.

49

'This is not a luxury hotel,' went Alia quiet. 'They may not speak English. But it is very convenient and I think it is good enough for you Nicky.'

They spoke English. Fact they spoke English better than a load of geezers up London. And for definite all the geezers up Scouser land.

They welcomed me to their country and their city and their hotel and probably their toilet. They yacked on to Alia in Urdu or maybe Punjabi round there, then they got down to the shekels in English. Alia doshed me beforehand so I never got showed up in public getting funded by a bird. They wanted cash up front and my passport. No problem. They filled out a dozen bits of paper. They welcomed me a bit more. Then they gave me a key and told me I was room 319.

'They show me the way or what?' I went quiet to Alia.

'No Nicky. In this hotel I think you have to find your own way. Probably someone will come along in a few minutes to show you how the television works.'

'Reckon I know how a TV works. Not too strong on the old sense of direction round the gaff though.'

'Room 319 will be on the third floor.'

'Yeah?'

'Trust me. The lift is over there. Take it to the third floor then just look around until you find it.'

'Sweet.'

'Oh, and Nicky, maybe the lights only work when you put the door key in a slot.'

'Yeah?'

'See you soon. I will wait here.' Case I ravished her soon as we got in the door.

I went for a recce. Ten minutes and I found the room. Even got the lights on.

They got TV and towels and a big bed and a big fan went whirring whenever you wanted. Telephone if I knew anyone I wanted to bell. Shower. Hot water. Better than home. Stay here and help out on the convalescence after the train journey. Fortnight without leaving the room ought to do the trick then I could go back up Walthamstow.

Knock on the door and a geezer came in polite. Brought the soap and toilet paper. Kind of useful. Showed me how a television worked, maybe reckoned we never got them in England yet. Stood there inside the door and thanked me. So I reckoned I better give him ten rupees. Not used to being a rich bastard.

I went back down the lobby where Alia was waiting.

'I thought you were lost,' she turned round and said. 'Is it all right? Will you be comfortable here?'

'No grief,' I went. 'Only missing a hot bird for sharing it with, know what I mean?' Then I sneezed a few times. 'Best you go out and do the business then Alia. I just lie here and snuff it. See you later.'

Only she carried on with the giggling again, no respect for a feller's pain. 'Now who is complaining?' she went. 'Who is Mr Traveller, eh? I will go off and see my family, Nicky, then we will all come back later to collect you and hope to find you alive. Is that all right? If you are in your room we will ring your bell from the lobby.'

'You can ring my bell any time Alia,' I turned round and said. Then I thought about it. 'Excepting now I reckon,' I goes. 'Bleeding bell ain't got any donger in it just the moment to my way of thinking. No lead in the old pencil Alia, you hear what I'm saying?'

She grinned without any pity at all. I went back and got under the shower then crept into their bed. Give Lahore a chance any day only you got to say it never made a good start.

I slept. Then I woke up.

All I knew was I got to get up their toilet. In their bathroom. I slid out the bed and found it.

Toilet stood there waiting for me. Only question was which end I put in it.

I knelt down and stuck my mush in it. Waiting for breakfast and lunch and last night's tea, all arriving the same time. Then I changed my mind about the end. Got up and sat on it instead.

Good decision. One second later half the world came out of my arse.

Then two seconds after that the other half came out my gob.

Tricky situation puking up through your legs. Got to take care or you get very messy.

Body emptied out, I got up and cleaned round. Alia gave me some bottles of water she bought on the station before we came up the hotel. I drank them all. Then I sicked them back up.

Then I went back to bed for a little snooze. Soon be right as rain no problem.

CHAPTER EIGHT

T HERE WAS A ringing going round in my bonce. There was a giant Scouser thick and hairy chasing me round the estate with a toilet round his neck and a bell in his paw.

'No no no!' I cried out. He came closer. I thrashed out at him. Knocked his bell over.

'Nicky?' went a voice. 'Nicky you all right?'

'Uh?'

'Nicky?'

It was a ringing ring only it was far far away. Either it was next door's dog and bone or I was Mutt and Jeff from the fever. Then I clocked it. Lying on the floor where I knocked it over. It was Alia belling me from downstairs.

'Alia?' I goes picking it up and croaking weak.

'Nicky you all right? You dying?'

'Yeah. I got serious trots. Serious I'm telling you.'

'Oh you poor thing Nicky.' Then she giggled. 'Nicky I think we had better come up and see you. I am with my uncle and my cousin. Are you decent?'

'Always a decent geezer Alia.'

'Oh do shut up. We will come up and see you in one minute.'

When they came I had my gob down that toilet again.

'Oh dear oh dear,' went Uncle. He stood at the doorway shaking his head. 'Sad case. Very sad case.'

'Nicky may I introduce you to Number One Uncle on the other side,' goes Alia. No name only Number One. 'And cousin Ramzan.' Ramzan was tall and kind of wispy, social worker type. Not a lot of assist in a spot of howsyourfather on heavy rock night down the Standard.

'Pleased to meet you,' we all goes together. Only difference was I was wiping puke off my gob and they weren't.

I flushed the toilet and got back in the bed. Walked across only wearing my underpants, hoped Alia never got insatiable.

'Very sad case,' Uncle went again. Alia giggled again. Hard woman. Never mopped my brow.

'I reckon you better come back in the morning Alia,' I goes feeble. 'When I'm dead.'

'We will bring you some water and diarrhoea pills,' she turned round and said. 'Tomorrow you will be better.'

'After I'm dead be much better.'

'Ramzan will get them for you now.' Ramzan went out the door. Still left Uncle for guarding her. 'Uncle will ask the hotel to look after you,' she went. 'He is very well respected in Lahore so they will keep a good eye on you.'

Uncle went out the door.

Alia and me were alone.

'Jesus Alia,' I went. 'You and me alone in a bedroom. You fancy a spot of nookie or what?'

'You have not shaved since we left London Nicky …'

'Soon put that right, be smooth as a baby's bum.'

'And you smell of sick …'

'Ah yeah. Bit more of a tough one.'

54

'Otherwise of course I would give up my virtue and my upbringing and my self-respect and my friendship with Noreen straight away Nicky.'

'How I was thinking Alia. How I was thinking. 'Scuse me a mo .. .' I got up out the bed sudden and I shut the bathroom door behind me on account of I felt the runs coming on again this time not the gob-job. I emptied out a bit more I never knew was there then came back in the bedroom.

'I think maybe you have been a little foolish with what you have been drinking Nicky. Do not drink the water out of this jug they give you here. Even I would not drink it and I am more used to it than you are. Drink only bottled water. And be very careful what you eat from now on, the spicy food.'

Giving me the lecture. Some birds might give a geezer a little sympathy.

'Likes a good curry back home Alia.'

'This is not home. Your food is safe in my family's home but outside there are flies everywhere.'

'Hear what you're saying.'

'And too many curries anyway can upset you. I should not have curry for breakfast if I were you.'

Shit. Thought of a curry for breakfast ...

'Ah. Here is cousin Ramzan. I shall introduce you once more because I am not sure you were concentrating properly the first time.'

'Very pleased to meet you,' goes Ramzan.

'All right mate?'

Ramzan brought the water and diarrhoea pills for my supper. I drank a couple of pints and swallowed half a dozen. Felt better already. Then he brought out the sweeties.

'Diazepam,' he goes.

'Pardon?'

'I have brought you some diazepam from the chemist to help you drowse a little.'

Jesus. Diazepam they gave the junkies in nick. On the street high value. Hard for getting them legal even on a prescription. Fortnight of them and I'd be clucking.

'How many mills?' I goes.

'Excuse me?'

'How many mills in each tablet?'

He checked the box. 'Er, fifty milligrammes in each I think.'

Holiday never looked so bad after all. Do a bit of flying. In prison they only gave the junkies five mills.

'Just one for starters,' I goes. 'Need to wake up tomorrow or the day after. Take one now I reckon please soon as you like.'

Number One Uncle came back in. 'I have talked to the staff,' he turned round and said. 'They will keep special eye on you. I have requested they advise me instantly on any sign of deterioration.'

'Cheers mate.'

'It is my pleasure. We are very sorry you cannot visit us tonight but we hope that tomorrow you will be fit as fiddle.'

'I hope so too Uncle. Very kind of you. Diazepam going to drift me along I reckon.'

They all shuffled out the door waving. Call me tomorrow. Alia turned round giggling. Hard woman.

So I was alone in Pakistan with the lurgy and a television and a few sleepers. Television only showing Urdu and cricket, did the same job as the sleepers only slower.

I went back to dreamland.

Puking up was nowhere near as bad on drugs. More like what my mate Sherry called an out of body experience. Out of

56

this body anyhow. Did a bit more retching then everything quietened down. All the time buzzing slightly. Only needed a pint of Pernod with it and I was well away. Trouble was Pakistan got a shortage of Pernod.

I slept fourteen hours if you included all that. No problem. Then when I was dozing nicely that bleeding bell went off again.

Found it and picked it up like a hero.

'Uh,' I went.

'Sir?'

'Uh?'

'Sir?'

Might go on a time this. 'Speaking,' I goes. 'Sir speaking I reckon.'

'Sir this is desk. You are still alive?'

'Not sure mate. How about you?'

'We are instructed to keep good eye on you. Very glad to hear you are still alive sir.'

'Thank you mate.'

'Is there anything you are requiring? Do you wish to have breakfast brought to your room?'

'I get a choice?'

'Of course sir. We have wide selection of breakfasts. There is choice of cornflakes or—'

'No mate, sorry and that. I got to eat up here or I get a choice on where I eat?'

'Yes sir you have choice of venue also. You can have room service or you can also eat in dining room of course sir if you are preferring.'

'Thank you geezer, I reckon you got a smart gaff here, know what I mean? Cheers and that, reckon I'll be down in two ticks.'

'In two ticks sir. Very pleased to hear you are alive.'

I got out of bed slow without being sick. I got in the shower cackling. Maybe on account of that or maybe it was the diazepam. I was so spacy I never even realised I was still stood under cold water until after about fifteen minutes it went hot. I was cackling again then.

I went downstairs ever so ever so slow.

Their dining room got a tablecloth. I held it for stopping me falling over. And that was when I was sitting down.

Waiter came up. Doshed me a menu.

'Chai,' I goes.

'Chai. Anything else?'

'Boiled eggs,' I goes. 'Boiled like there's no tomorrow. Boiled like there ain't nothing left.'

'Yes. Hard-boiled eggs.'

'Do me nicely no problem.'

'No problem.'

He brought the tea straight off. I sipped it black. Then they brought the hard-boiled eggs. I gobbed them slowly.

Got the answer. Black tea and hard-boiled eggs.

Sharon and me we were never sick when we were kids except Mondays. Then we got serious ill. You never did want school agg after a hard bit of weekend whizzing.

We started Friday night. Not a lot of geezers let their kid sister come clubbing with them only Sharon was a good 'un. Twelve years old and never even got cream crackered. We kept her on a ration mind. Few Es and a bit of straight whizz for keeping her going, never enough so she couldn't stop at the end. We reckoned it was for her health anyhow, keep her off the glue like the rest round that time. Me and Jimmy and Wayne liked a bit of acid with it, not too often though. Used a spot of coke when we got it, not too easy scoring when you weren't allowed in pubs. Mostly we traded it for car radios up the snooker hall.

So Sharon came up the club down Clapton with us Fridays. Looked eighteen older than us so no problem, anyway we never drank alcohol only water when we were racing. We stepped in whenever some geezer got leery with her on the dance floor. Told them how old she was, even back then they heard about child abuse. Three o'clock we sent her home in a cab on account of she needed her beauty sleep and also the stabbings started then. Eight o'clock we got some breakfast then had to lift a motor for getting home seeing as cabbies never would take us. One week Old Bill sat there outside on observation so we had to take a bus. Never again.

We stayed up all Saturday morning then went down West Ham for a rucking in the afternoon. Evening time went to bed a few hours then up at two thirty for catching the prime time clubbing again. Time we stopped it was Sunday night. Hardly expect a geezer to go to school after a weekend like that so we laid behind.

Mum came up shouting sometimes Mondays when she could be arsed so that was where the sickness came in. We kept a stock of salt in the bathroom and poured it in each other's gobs. Then we stuck fingers down each other's tonsils. Time Mum came in we were puking nicely.

Since those days I never was ill till now except when I got proper pissed up.

It was a new experience.

CHAPTER NINE

O N THE TABLE they got four curries all different. Then rice and dal and yoghurt and nan. Kind of a snack for when you got peckish round early afternoon.

Eight sitting down. Number One Uncle and his missis. Ramzan and his brother Sammy and his sister got no name. Another geezer, maybe number two uncle. Alia and me.

Alia started cackling even before she clocked me going greener.

'Nicky will this be enough food for you?' she went. 'Are you very hungry today? Shall I help you to this beautiful aubergine dish?'

'Urrk,' I turned round and said.

'How is your digestion today Nicky?' went Uncle. 'You are still not looking very well I am thinking, although a little better than yesterday when you were being so sick and having such diarrhoea.'

''Scuse me Uncle,' I goes. 'Reckon your nosh looks like Al grub, go down a bleedin' treat in some takeaway on Hoe St only I still got a touch of the old howsyourfather, you get my meaning? 'Scuse me again don't want to diss you only you got any hard-boiled eggs in the gaff? You hear what I'm saying?'

'Hard-boiled eggs,' goes his missis. 'Of course. Of course.'

They never got servants round this side the family so missis had to go off the kitchen herself. Fortunate they got a stock in, she came back in ten seconds with four hard-boiled eggs. I started on them slow.

'You will be egg-bound,' whispers Alia next to me.

'What I'm hoping Alia. Chance'd be a fine thing.'

We chatted kind of polite. I tried for pulling the sister only whenever you got closer than ten yards she dived in the kitchen. Bit of a looker in the bargain. I kept on giving her the glances.

Then they started yacking about Kamran. Why we were here.

'Yes he came,' goes Uncle. 'He came to pay his respects naturally. He stayed here two nights. We still have small bag upstairs. I think he left most of his things with Other Side in Karachi. Then he disappeared from us. We were thinking he had gone to Jhelum maybe for visiting family. But we rang them after few days and he was not there. It is mystery. Very worrying. Kamran is such good boy never in any trouble. We do not know what to do. We have heard nothing. At first we thought you hear something in England but now we know you do not.'

'Nothing at all you heard?' goes Alia.

'Nothing at all.'

Alia already told me they went over the story all night. Now like family conference they did it again considering my benefit.

'Do you think we should go to Jhelum?' went Alia. 'Or should we stay longer in Lahore and ask around?'

'I think you should stay in Lahore. Now we know that we know nothing. We shall ask everywhere. It is big city but it is small town if you understand me. Two three days and we shall find out something I am sure.'

'All right,' goes Alia. 'That suit you Nicky?'

'Suit me no problem. Put a stopper in the old plughole by then I reckon.'

They all looked kind of pleased. Treated me to the smiles and niceness like I was their main man, Charlie Big Potatoes and no messing. Good as gold that family. My mum ought to take a butcher's. Sitting round passing the grub and not yelling. Never happened round Priory Court. And no-name daughter even gave me the smirk. Only a pity their families never let the birds out to play.

Then they came up with the heart-stopper. All going hunky-dory till then.

'Nicky, do you have a wife at home?' goes Uncle sudden.

'Eh?'

'Or are you engaged? Fiancée?'

'Er, not rightly Uncle. Er, like there's some bird ...'

Bleeding Alia getting her rocks off cackling quiet pretending she was choking.

'Some what?'

'Like, well, know how it is Uncle, geezers and that ...'

'No wife? No fiancée?' They all clocked each other like Walthamstow got to be a disaster area. 'No wife?' goes missis. 'No fiancée?' goes Uncle Two. They all shook their Judge Dreads sympathetic. 'Tut tut tut,' goes Uncle One. 'Very sad case.'

'Not too sad,' I turned round and said. 'Not too sad Uncle. Bit young and that, know what I mean?'

'You want that we find you a wife? Nice girl good family?'

'Yes, find you a wife,' they all go. 'Nice girl good family.'

''Scuse me everyone,' I goes. ''Scuse me I reckon I got to use your toilet again.' I went out the door kind of hasty.

* * *

Not long after we came out their door led through the yard to the back doubles. Me and Alia and Ramzan.

'You want a wife Nicky?' goes Alia cackling fit to bust her underwear. 'You want us to find a nice girl for you about nineteen? Probably very clever girl just your type, got four A-levels and all she wants to do in an evening is study for the university? You just say the word Nicky and we will all go ahead for you.'

'It would be a pleasure,' Ramzan turned round and said serious. 'My family would be honoured to do all they can.'

Ramzan came out with me and Alia on security duty, escort us down the town. It seemed like they missed out on that point when they wanted a match-up, how the whole of Pakistan was never keen on their birds knocking off white geezers. We were coming out for a taxi or rickshaw for taking me back up my hotel. I was feeling kind of queasy, what with the gut job and the yacking about weddings.

We got in the alley minding no one's business only ours.

Three geezers standing there with rifles.

'All right fellers?' I goes.

They went something in Urdu. Not too sure what it was only I caught their drift on account of how they pointed their shooters at me. They got a serious attitude.

'No need for being like that John,' I goes to the closest one. I went up and clocked him nice and friendly. Then I smacked him on the hooter with a headbutt, proper High St special.

I was never very fucking useful with the old headbutt only this one went down a treat. I reckon they never got them up Pakistan so he never expected it. His hooter spread out lovely, gravy everywhere. He probably caught my cold in the bargain. Other two geezers so surprised they never moved. I picked my feller's blade out of the holder on his waist and cut the second one sharp across his gun arm.

63

Alia picked up the idea. Ramzan standing around wondering what the fuck only Alia was brought up better. She whacked the third geezer in the problem area so he doubled up gasping fast.

First two dropped their shooters and legged it. I wanted one for a pet though. Put the boot in on the gasping geezer, left him curled.

'Ramzan mate,' I goes. 'You never got the hang of this game. You got to get in there early doors, no point waiting for the whistle or they shoot you innit? Never last on the streets of Walthamstow, know what I mean?'

'Quite right Nicky,' goes Alia. 'Far too polite Ramzan. You have to go for it.'

Ramzan standing there rooted. Then he comes over to me confidential.

'Nicky,' he goes quiet.

'Ramzan.'

'Do you know, she hit that man in … in … in his private parts.'

'Always best for a bird Ramzan, you hear what I'm saying? Get in there sharp. Woomph.'

'But how did she know where they were? She is not married. Was it an accident do you think?'

'Probably Ramzan. Or else it was GCSE biology. Now we drag this fucker in your yard, you with me?'

'What will we do with him there?'

'What the Old Bill do. Spot of heavy questioning.'

'Questioning?'

'Questioning. You keep your mum and dad out the way so Alia and I do some serious asking. How you get information innit? Feller got to be expecting it, don't want to disappoint him.'

'What do we do with the guns?'

'Fuck knows. Chuck 'em. Me I'm not too bad with a sticker, fuckin' useless with a shooter. Pawn them my advice, take 'em down the thrift.'

Three of us dragged him in their yard.

'Nicky,' goes Alia, 'what do we do if he talks straight away? Do we still give him that heavy questioning?'

'Got to be a bit disappointing he does, Alia. Still question him a little, know what I mean? Never want to leave him go regardless.'

She walked all the way round him, gave him the gaze.

'So how do we start?' she went.

'You just keep on stamping on his bollocks. I work away with the blade. You ask him a few questions in Urdu.' I put the blade next the feller's hooter, let him clock it close up.

Turned out then the geezer was a squealer anyhow, got no bottle. Ramzan went in the house and we got to work. Two minutes and he gabbed. I never even cut his hooter that much, least not on the outside.

He squawked.

'What's he say?' I asked.

'He hasn't said much yet Nicky. I think your knee is too hard on his neck. Let him loose a little bit.'

I eased up an inch. 'Now what's he say?'

He squawked again.

'He says Kamran is in Karachi.'

'Karachi!'

'Karachi.'

'We just fucking got here from Karachi!'

'He says Kamran has been kidnapped.'

'Kidnapped?'

'He says they kidnapped him. He says they were hired by a man from Karachi. They kidnapped him here in Lahore then the man's own men took him back to Karachi.'

65

'Why's he still hanging round here then?' Feller was grunting a bit under me. I wasn't sure he was going to croak or trying for a getaway. I let him up a fraction for breathing then poked around inside his hooter with the blade, let him know I was around.

'They were paid to keep an eye open up here and report on anything that happened. I think they took it into their own hands to confront us.'

'Why'd they hit Kamran up here instead of Karachi?'

'I can tell you the answer to that one Nicky. Everyone knows. It is getting too hot for kidnappers in Karachi because of government measures. They probably targeted him there and found out where he was going, then decided to make their move up here. They may even make ransom demands up here as well to conceal his real whereabouts.'

'What's the name of his boss man?'

She asked him. He kept tight.

'Stamp on his bollocks.'

She stamped on his bollocks.

'Jamil Khan Jamal!'

'No problem feller. That name mean anything to you Alia?'

'Not to me Nicky.'

'You reckon it's straight up?'

She stamped again. Geezer cried out.

'He says it is true. Jamil Khan Jamal is a very dangerous man. This man here could be dead now for grassing up the boss man.'

'What you reckon we do with him?'

'Let him go Nicky. He will not talk about us I think.'

'Hear what you're saying.'

We let him go. He scrabbled away dripping gravy. Three separate paths of gravy leading off.

We took their rifles indoors. Someone had to find a use for them.

CHAPTER TEN

I POPPED UP The Mall. Needed to send my mum a post-card. Sent Noreen one instead.

'Wish you were here,' I went. 'Instead of me.'

Post office was bigger than Walthamstow Town Hall. I walked round ten minutes before I found the counter. Queued up polite like. After twenty geezers pushed in front of me I sussed I was never doing it right. One other geezer was still in the queue in front. Just when he got up the counter I shoved him out the way.

'Stamp for Walthamstow,' I goes. 'E17.'

Feller looked at the picture on my card. Then he turned it over and read what I got to say. Then he stamped it on the machine so Noreen never got a proper stamp for Pakistan.

'Cheers,' I went. 'Hope it gets there quick.'

'Inshallah,' he goes.

The Mall was wide as a football pitch. Farmer driving goats along it looking for bits of green. Mercs and BMWs cruising. Donkey carts cruising. Outside the post office some geezer was brewing up by the side of the road. He got cups bigger than a thimble, smaller than an eggcup.

'All right geezer?' I goes cheery.

'Salaam,' he goes.

'Chai,' I goes fluent.

'No problem,' he goes.

I doshed him five rupees. Tea was still thick and sweet. The time I drank six of them I was ready for anything. They reckoned I got to go sightseeing up Anarkali for bargains. End of The Mall and fork right. So I did.

All kinds of gear they got. I was after some shirts and that for Danny. Little shops like a car boot sale. I picked up a check number about Danny's size.

'How much feller?' I went.

'How much you want to pay?'

This never took us forward. I moved off.

He came after. 'One hundred rupees!' he went.

I kept on going.

'Ninety!' he turned round and said.

I reckoned I found a bargaining tactic here. Carried on.

'Eighty-five!'

I turned round on seventy. Got a nice little item for Danny under a quid. So I bought another five.

I bought a bag for putting them in. Then I stepped out the shop and some dude was waiting for offering me. Little slinky feller wearing jeans.

'Mister,' he goes.

'All right?'

'You are from England?'

'Walthamstow.'

'You want hashish?'

Couple of spliffs take all the pain away.

'You reckon I got to be a Scouser?' I went.

'Excuse me?'

'You reckon I came down off the fucking Christmas tree or what?'

'For you I make very good price. Because I like you.'

'Fuckin' generous mate. Now you can fuck off. Fuckin' fuck off you got me?'

Always some chance the geezer was legit. About as much chance as me sprouting wings. Bit more chance he was a fucking grasser, do the fucking deal and whoops there's six Old Bill round the corner. Twenty years in a Pakistani peter. On the street? You got to be making joke here having a laugh.

In some bookshop they got the Maths books we had in school. I still couldn't do the bleeding sums. I bought a story about Lahore by some bird called Bapsi for the journey, not a lot of sex and violence still pass the time. I went over Pizza Hut and got a bit of solid take-away. Put it in the napkin for a few days later when the eggs ran out. Then I shanked it back up the hotel for a little snooze and some more pills.

Alia and me after we whacked the geezers we discussed how we were getting back up Karachi. We discussed it about two seconds. Then we reckoned we were flying. No more trains.

So she was off getting our tickets and she reckoned she'd pick me up in three hours.

I went downstairs sitting in the lobby waiting for Alia and clocking the action. Young geezer kind of serious came over wanting to yack about his career structure.

'Come again?' I goes.

'I have a degree in biochemistry and a Masters in computers,' he turned round and said. 'I am hoping you can advise me on my future career structure in terms of education.'

'No problem. Get it sorted John.'

'You see my special difficulty is area of study. Both the subject and the geographical area you understand. For my PhD.'

'Course.'

'Yes my course. Please excuse me for interrupting you like this. You see I have an offer from Laredo, Texas and an offer from Canberra, Australia but I was considering taking my next step in London. Perhaps you could advise me about the various colleges at your university in London. You may have some knowledge of teaching quality, accommodation, costs, you understand? You are from London?'

'Walthamstow geezer.'

'Walthamstow …' He looked kind of curious like he never heard of it.

'They got a college in Walthamstow natural.'

'Yes? And this college is part of London University? It is not a college I have heard of I must confess.'

'Walthamstow part of London no question. So the college got to be part of that university innit?'

He came over sort of doubtful.

'And this Walthamstow, it is good area?'

'Serious.'

'Serious. That is good. Serious area. You think it is good for study for a PhD?'

'No worries mister.' Some kind of chemist's most likely.

'For my doctorate you understand.'

'Ah well. Say no more mate. All our doctors are Asians in Walthamstow. You be like a pig in shit.'

'Pig?'

Oh Gawd. Even I reckoned you never mentioned pigs round Muslims. Fortunate just then before I got to make my excuses in comes Alia.

'Ah Nicky. Very nice to see you making friends,' she turned round and said. 'Your health must be improving.'

70

'Feller wanting to go to Walthamstow college,' I went. 'Be a doctor. They do that at Walthamstow like a City and Guilds or what?'

'No Nicky they do not do that at Walthamstow. Are you sure it was Walthamstow?'

'Walthamstow sounds very nice place,' goes the geezer. 'Good area for serious study.'

'Walthamstow is full of young men like Nicky,' Alia turned round and said. Then the geezer went something in Urdu. Then she went something in Urdu. Then he went pale and started to quiver.

'Now then Nicky are you packed?' Alia goes to me. 'Our plane leaves in one hour.'

'Hour!'

'One hour. Are you packed?'

'Packed!'

'Stop repeating everything I say and move quickly.'

'Alia, I move quick and we got a serious health problem here I'm telling you.'

'Nicky, there is a taxi waiting and all my bags packed inside. Two minutes you get my meaning?'

I was up the room and back two minutes packed my toothbrush Danny's shirts and all my pills. We were out that door like a fruit curry. Alia squared up the hotel. Outside she got a cowboy waiting in his wagon and shotgun leaning out the other window, Speedy Gonzales and his cousin Hopalong. We went down the hotel ramp at sixty and hit the street with a dust storm. Alia promised them double fare we caught the plane.

She never promised extra for being alive so Speedy never gave too much thinking to that one. I dented the top of my bonce where it bumped the roof thirty times. Five minutes and I covered up total and clocked the floor, best I never knew what hit me.

We made it thirty-five minutes to spare. We went in their airport breezing.

They were all waiting for us cussing on account of we were twenty-five minutes from departure time. Cussed me out seeing as it was bad manners for cussing a bird.

'No problem John,' I goes to the feller kind of cool. 'Sorry to diss you and that being late, still we climb on the old hopper innit? Still waiting on the platform am I right or it pissed off home or what then?'

Geezer turned to Alia seemed like he never understood. Alia did a spot of translation and he was happy enough. Anyhow all the rest the passengers turned up the same time as we did or a bit later. Ten minutes before kick-off seemed like standard time for checking in round there.

We got back up Karachi and it was hot. Hotter than Lahore. Hotter than last time we were there. Hotter than Walthamstow twice over. Hot.

CHAPTER ELEVEN

'THERE IS ONE difference,' went Mr Hanid, 'between European criminal and Asian.'

'Yeah?'

'European criminal when they are arrested they tell you everything straight away. Like that.'

'Not round my manor they never.'

'One time I catch European gun smugglers. They tell me they are guilty immediately!'

'Got to be Germans mate.'

'While Asian criminals they prefer to tell you later after the torture.'

'Torture?' I went.

* * *

We were sat in the Oasis. We were under a parasol so geezers in uniform brought us drinks. Alia never let me drink fruit juice nor have ice on account of she reckoned I suffered enough in the trot region for one trip. So everyone else sucked away through their straws and I sipped away on the black tea.

Smooth geezers played tennis and a couple of dads in the pool with kids. No birds in there with skimpy bikinis, spoiled the point of pools to my way of thinking. Women in the long gear chatting under the umbrellas. Rich people's club the Oasis and the women were allowed out chatting other rich people. Couple of white women covered in the bargain so I never got a flash of flesh. First white women I clocked since I left England, just beginning to wonder they all dropped off.

You could get to like rich bastards, sipping and chatting and servants bringing out the drinks. Only a pity it was never a few Pernods and a jump-up later. I had to make do with thinking on the Pernod and getting downwind a bit of perfume off the women.

And just in case you got careless after a bit of perfume you clocked hubbie and the help waiting to slice you when you put the feelers in.

It was coming on evening how we sat there, getting dark and the mosquitoes out for a night bite. Get rid of the trots and go home with malaria most likely.

Inspector Hanid carried on yacking. No stopping him once you wound his clock. Alia brought me down the club for meeting him. He was kind of a chief of police. Friend of the family. Least that was one way of looking at it. Other way was he owed them and they happened to mention he better get down there. We sat there sipping quiet while he gave out the SP on the form round Karachi police work.

'You understand the torture?' he went like it was computer classes.

'Catch your drift mister. Like you're partial to a bit now and then, right?'

'We like to torture a little, yes. How else we get results? But it is all quite harmless of course. And we are very careful. No marks.'

'Course not. Between neck and knee innit?'

'Ah! I see you are expert.'

'On the receiving end a few times down some cell.'

'And the soles of the feet naturally.'

'Natural.'

'But you see it is specially necessary because of my present job. I am liaison officer between main police force and ANF.'

'ANF?'

'Anti Narcotics Force.'

'Get your meaning.'

'Where we have to give them damn good whacking. Although sometimes it is not necessary, because now I have found an even more successful torture.'

Alia looking green about the gills. Inspector never noticed.

'It is alcohol torture …'

'Alcohol?'

'We are getting excellent results with this alcohol torture. We give them couple pints of alcohol and they talk like bloody parrot!'

Alia and me we clocked each other. Brain starting to go into high revs.

'They do?' I goes wondering.

'Information coming out of their arses!'

'Er, any special kind of alcohol? Pint of lager like?'

'They make this alcohol in village. Make it from vegetables you understand. They sell it you know the people. We arrest them, keep alcohol in police station. Very horrible stuff.'

'True words mister. Hate you give it to me.'

'Of course.'

'Although prepared to do my bit in the war against drugs course. Guinea pig type thing you need a taster.'

'Then we add mandrax to the alcohol.'

Jesus. Mandrax, old-time barbs. My mum's generation all the junkies did mandrax.

'Then we keep them standing up with no darkness for two or three days and they tell us all we want and they even make things up to keep us happy and maybe incriminate more people!'

'Pure grass seed innit?'

'You are a gangster?' he goes sudden.

'Nah mate. More of the small time. Ex. Retired. Noreen my missis she put the mockers on all that. These days takes me all my time slicing a radish. Not gangster style.'

'Ah.' He was kind of disappointed. 'I heard you were wanting my assistance to talk about Pakistan big criminals. Maybe I was thinking it was for setting up here yourself.'

Jesus. He was wanting a backhander. Grease my way.

Alia went something in Urdu. Then something more. Then the family joined in. Making out our intentions.

'Ah,' went the inspector. 'You are wanting to talk about kidnapping. Then I can indeed help. I am man for job.' He smiled happy for helping.

'Right on.'

'You see kidnapping and drugs are linked in Pakistan. There is linkage.'

'Linkage.'

'Strong linkage. Same people often involved and for same reasons. Money. Power. Politics. And I can give you the name of someone I know through my work who can sort you out. Have no doubt.'

'Be doing us a favour mister. Got to be we owe you one. Only want some geezer tell us where our mate is, see how we get him back home like.'

76

'I can give you introduction to Abdul Hafeez.'

All the family went whoosh like someone just died.

They came up giving me more of the black tea and the inspector more cashews. Him and me we were understanding each other now like we went to school together.

Only he needed time for getting round the point. Give the geezer half an inch and he was off round the old houses again.

'We are winning this battle against drugs you know,' he went.

'Yeah course mate.' And I just clocked a pig flying past. Police winning the battle back home in the bargain. Soon be no one using except the whole population.

'But we have interim problems.'

'Just like Walthamstow mister. Interim problems.'

'When Russians invaded Afghanistan all drug merchants came down to Pakistan over pass. Now they grow their poppies near Peshawar. Karachi is natural outlet for them. And they have Kalashnikovs and SMGs and all the bloody armoury you know.'

'Hear what you're saying.'

'Then they buy up politicians.'

'Yeah?'

'Politicians all bloody liars and criminals. Same your country same here. All bloody criminals. We catch these drug merchants and what is happening? Bloody politicians tell us we are letting them go. Or they fix bloody trials. We try. Bloody police try. No good.'

'Same old story innit? Do your best. Dice loaded before kick-off.'

'You understand. And if we catch politicians red-handed with drug merchants we are not even allowed torture!'

'Nah!'

'I am telling you! Order of judge, special court order every time when we catch politicians. No torture. Always health grounds. Very sick men politicians.'

'Never credit it. All bent, know what I mean? Police good as gold. All them others bent.'

'Police we are trying to do good job. Good as gold I hear you say. That is us. All others corrupt.'

Alia sitting there like she might bust a gut.

'Mr Hanid——' she went.

'Stay cool girl,' I went. Not very likely he listen to a bird anyhow.

'Mr Hanid——'

'Now Inspector,' I carries on. Alia got to be reckoning it just a faint possibility he never got his Volvo we clocked outside the gate off his inspector's whack. In the bargain she just earholed him making me an offer two minutes earlier. So I stepped in quick just in case he might take notice. 'Now Inspector,' I goes. 'Appreciate meeting you, and you like making over all this info' and that. You reckon you were saying how drugs and kidnapping there got to be a connection?'

He paused kind of reflecting. He chewed on his cashews.

'Whenever there is big bucks,' he turned round and said, 'there is connection. And kidnapping there was big bucks.'

'Was?'

'Was big bucks. Now there is still big bucks but not so easy to get. We are winning battle against kidnapping. So they turn to drugs. Same people of course.'

'Yeah?' I goes. 'You winning both them battles? Battle against kidnapping, that like your battle against drugs?'

'No. Not like battle against drugs.' Then he kind of giggled. Winked and leaned forward then he tapped his hooter like we were in this together him and me, except all the others heard just like I did. 'This battle against kidnapping,' he goes.

'This battle we are truly winning. Other battle is all lies you understand. This battle we win because we have bloody CPLC!'

Every time he told me a bit more it turned out there was a bit more he never told me yet.

'CPLC?' I went.

'Yes, CPLC.'

'What it is?'

'Committee. For Citizens. For Police. For Liaison.'

'Get your meaning. And what it does?'

'Liaison. Police—'

'Yeah I ain't thick mate. I caught on that bit. What it does, this liaison thingy?'

'Bastards take over from police on kidnapping cases. Catch bloody kidnappers. Police never catch kidnappers. Bastard CPLC catch bloody kidnappers, make police look bloody stupid.'

'Got to be hard that.'

'Police have no resources you understand. No men. No money. No technology. Then come along bastard CPLC. They give them telephones and computers and money and men. They catch bloody kidnappers!'

We all clocked each other round the table.

'It is true,' goes uncle sipping his cool drink cool. 'It is all true. We have arranged to talk to CPLC next. After tea with Inspector Hanid we have CPLC for dinner.'

Inspector was never a happy bunny over this. He looked like his granny died or he lost all his bribe dosh. Not only he never got the resources, he never got dinner neither.

Then he brightened up considerable when we got the ransom demand.

Waiter came out with a silver tray. On the tray he got a letter.

'One crore dollars,' it went. 'US.'

Only it was in paper cuttings. In English. It went like 'one CRORE dollars. us.'

Meant fuck all to me only all the rest went shit-faced.

'You more letters,' it carried on. Either they never spoke English too good or they got a shortage of words they wanted. 'No contact police. He die. More orders. Wait.'

Then another sentence like an afterthought. 'Not talk CPLC. He die.'

Then what they were getting round to saying again like a repeater. 'One CRORE dollars. US. He die.'

They made their moves.

'They know we are here now at the club,' went cousin Rashid.

'They have followed us,' went uncle.

Atmosphere round that table dropped like West Ham just got relegated. No use pointing out they could get promoted again next season. No use pointing out Kamran seemed like he was still alive. They all knew where he was now and it was never like time for celebration.

And one crore dollars.

'One crore dollars?' I went. 'Alia?'

'One crore is one hundred thousand.'

'Lot of dosh,' I goes.

'And how do we know that they have truly got Kamran in their hands?' goes uncle. 'How do we know it is not an evil conspiracy just because they have heard that he is missing and we are making enquiries?'

'There anything else in that envelope?' I went.

Looked like there was a small lump of something tucked away like a midgy smoke of rock.

Uncle shook it out on the table by the cashews.

Then we all knew straight off. Always do a DNA test we wanted to be sure.

Recognise it anywhere. It was a little bit of ear.

CHAPTER TWELVE

WE ALL MOVED outside their club for the motors. Dudes in uniform brought them by the door. Mighty hush fell down. Far as I was concerned there were worse bits you could lose than a bit of lug. From where they were sitting though it seemed like a problem.

While we went through the club the inspector was picking up cashews off every table. When we got to the door he pulled me.

'You want contact,' he went. 'Abdul Hafeez.'

'Kind of handy,' I went. 'Geezer with attitude am I right?'

'He is brigand.'

'Reckon we got a few brigands round Walthamstow. Know the moves.'

'I make introduction you help me.'

'Help you? Bung you a fuckin' drink you meaning?'

'I am liking Swiss francs very much.'

I made with the close encounters. 'Gimme the fuckin' intro,' I went.

He passed me a bit of paper.

'They will want everything official through bloody CPLC,' he turned round and said. 'Official way is not always best way for results. Abdul Hafeez is unofficial.'

'Official and unofficial,' I went. 'Good combo innit? Do it proper then when that don't get a result do it natural. Say no more John.'

We went out in the car park. They were all shaking now they digested their news. Alia was in bits.

'Nicky this is worse than I feared,' she went crumpling at the edges. 'What the hell are we going to do? I should never have mixed you up in this, it is a police thing, I'm sorry. God, I don't know what Kamran is going through.'

'He got through secondary at McEntee, Alia. Anyone got through McEntee can handle a spot of kidnapping. Break his way out I reckon, have it on his toes.'

'The family will be visited by the CPLC this evening,' she went. 'Do you want to be there?'

'Never miss it.'

We went back home in all their motors.

Family was in mourning. Not only Kamran was family, they reckoned he was their guest up Pakistan and they were responsible and he got lifted. All down to them. They were never seeing it logical. The way I clocked it, happen in Pakistan happen up Walthamstow happen round the North Pole. Except not so many geezers up the North Pole. Happen almost anywhere, always heavy duty geezers.

They got a meal only three courses on account of their depression. I got the same course as normal. They never yacked at all except for business about kidnapping. Then after chow they got their visit off the man from the Pru.

He was very Charlie Big Potatoes indeed. In the bargain he gave Alia a very serious itch. Even when her bro got ear damage she still had her a serious itching problem round the geezer from the CPLC.

82

He gave us all his card. He was called Imran Khan. Vice president CPLC.

Even I was knowing there was a big noise in Pakistan called Imran Khan so I reckoned this got to be him. I never knew Pakistan was full of Imran Khans so first off I only thought Alia fancied him for his cricket playing.

He was never a real bingo in the looks department only he got long lashes and black eyes and cheeks like a baby's bum. He wore a safari suit never came off the market. He got lips for licking with.

And he was cool as a dip in the River Lea.

'I am so sorry to hear of your distress,' he turned round and said to the family. And me. And the servants. 'I hope we can be of service to you. The CPLC is here to help the whole of society.' He spoke all in English being polite and cool.

'Please tell us,' went Uncle. 'Tell us more about CPLC. Of course we know what it is but tell us where you fit in and what can you do?'

'You see,' went old Imran, 'you all know there was a major problem with kidnapping.'

'True,' they all went.

'Until recently there were three kidnappings every week. And no one could stop them. As you know the police had two difficulties preventing them succeeding in this battle. First, they had no computers. Second, they are very stupid.'

'True,' they all went.

Imran turned round for my benefit. 'In Pakistan you see,' he goes on, 'police are taken from the very poor and not educated classes. And the very stupid classes. They are paid badly. They cannot solve crises.'

'True,' they all went again.

'Same as back home,' I goes.

'Then if they do solve crises they are ordered by politicians to let the criminals go because the criminals pay the politicians.'

'Yes yes!'

'So we had a major problem with kidnapping which could only be solved by concerned citizens. And by direct government.'

'Direct government?' I goes quick before the chorus kicked in.

'Direct government from Islamabad. All the power was taken away from local government in Karachi. The constitution allows central government to do this for six months.'

'Right.'

'So they brought in direct government. They asked people like myself to join the CPLC. And they gave us computers.'

'So you ain't the filth?'

'No, I am not the police. I have a manufacturing business. I do not receive any payment for my work here. I look on it as my duty.'

Alia's little mince pies going wider and wider. Wedding bells were ringing up in threes whenever you pulled her handle.

'Now we do many things in the CPLC but we began with kidnapping, the most pressing problem. First we had to learn the skills necessary, both to track down the kidnappers and to negotiate with them. We worked very hard and we made some mistakes at first but finally we have achieved most of our objects. The result is that we have caught fifty per cent of all perpetrators of kidnapping. And the crime itself has fallen by ninety per cent in one year. At this moment we are dealing with only three kidnappings in the whole of the Karachi area. A year ago it might have been thirty.'

'Fellers can't hardly make a living,' I went.

'Exactly. And the rich can once again sleep smoothly in their beds.'

They all smiled.

Then they remembered their Kamran. Old Imran looked round at them waiting for the SP. 'Yes?' he went gentle.

Alia was the one for telling the business.

'Jamil Khan Jamal!' she went.

When her words came out her gob it was like they pulled the plug.

'I beg your pardon?' went old Imran.

'That is the man we believe to have taken Kamran.'

'Oh dear. I am sorry to hear that. Why do you think this?'

'Because a man in Lahore told us. A man who attacked us when we were making enquiries there.'

'A man attacked you? What happened? Were you hurt? How were you rescued?'

'Nicky gave him a High Street special. What he calls it. The man's nose was broken. Then Nicky nearly killed him. His friends ran off. Then he told us Kamran was kidnapped by Jamil Khan Jamal.'

Old Imran was taking in all this news. While Alia was gabbing like Hissing Sid on account of how Imran was giving her the hots he was gawping at us.

'You tackled Jamil Khan Jamal's sepoys?' he went. 'That is very unwise. Please promise me one thing if they should make any contact in the future. You will liaise with me immediately.'

'Of course,' went Alia. They never asked me. I reckoned we liaised all right that time.

'I would like very close liaison with you from the start.'

'Of course,' went Alia gooey.

'I shall start making enquiries tonight. When you hear anything at all you must call me immediately. When they telephone I need to be there if possible. Do not – I repeat not – make any arrangements with them independently. I must sanction any action. We must catch these people.'

'Of course,' went Alia. It was like no one else was in the room.

Then he turned to the rest. 'Do not tell them that the CPLC is involved,' he went. 'None of you please.'

'No!'

'Or I fear they will damage him seriously.'

I made him right on that one old Imran. What I'd do anyhow.

'But never fear.' He gave it cheese. 'Never fear for your brother, nephew, cousin. We shall find him and return him to you in the end.'

He was like a social worker with menaces. Except he dressed better than all the social workers I ever got.

In my time I witnessed some serious slicings round the old fifth gear.

When we were kids up McEntee you often got bored in science or art. Took the oppo while you got the tools for making some kid bleed. Best way was off the ear. Bleed a fucking bucket and not a lot of real damage.

Not always the way the teachers reckoned it though, globs of gravy all over the shop. I got school books round my mum's still stained with Jimmy Foley. Jimmy always took it like a geezer, stopped blubbing by the time we got home.

That was never serious slicing though, we were always leaving the situation in one piece. Serious slicing you got later round the clubs or in youth custody.

Most celebrity slicer in our borough was old Rameez.

Rameez was kind of a baron. Kind of a minor baron. He did local business, protection and retail and a bit of car theft. Position Rameez was in, he got muscle to do his dirty washing for him. No need for him to get his fingers dirty. Rameez

86

though he just had to get involved. Whatever way you clocked it, he just loved a spot of slicing.

Slice you soon as you clocked his blonde bit of stuff or spilled his drink or cut him in traffic when he was cruising his motor. Especially you overtook him in Forest Rd everyone watching. Next set of lights you found you got a sticker up your hooter. Aggravate him serious and he was up for a bit of scalping. Scalping he loved even better than slicing.

Up youth custody though was slicers' paradise. Most times they never even got a proper reason. Get in the wrong crowd or turn down an offer, next you know they got a blade stuck in a toothbrush and you had a visit round your cell off half a dozen of matey's mates. First offence slice your cheek. Twice I clocked half an earhole going down the drain. Youth custody never was a walk in the park.

So I never got so fussed like the rest for finding a touch of Kamran's fifth in the post. He got plenty left was how I reckoned it. Next stop was half a finger be a bit more hurtful.

CHAPTER THIRTEEN

A LIA TOOK ME back up the hotel with only a couple of aunts for minders who never spoke English good.

'Oh Nicky,' she goes.

'Yeah?' I goes. She sounded like ready for a legover. Breathing deep. Tonsils heaving. Could be my lucky day.

'Oh what a wonderful man,' she goes.

'Yeah?'

'All services totally free.'

'True,' I went.

'Imran Khan.'

Not me it turned out. Old Imran as it goes. She got the panting bosom for Imran on account of his smooth cheeks and his free services and maybe his manufacturing business.

'You got the serious hots Alia,' I turned round and said.

'It is not how I would describe my feelings Nicky. He is a very fine man. I believe he comes from a good family. But ... but ...'

It never took much to guess the rest.

'But nobody let on if he got a missis already!' I goes.

'Nicky you must find out!'

'Who, me?'

'No, I am sorry. My thoughts are running away with me. I shall speak to my aunts.'

We were nearly by the hotel.

'You OK about them hots?' I asked.

'Pardon Nicky?'

'You never want to be working them off? Scratch the itch type of thing? Know what I mean?'

'Nicky! I am a friend of Noreen!'

'Pretend you ain't?'

'How can you suggest such a thing?'

I reckoned she was halfway there. Got a serious itch.

'I am a Muslim!'

I carried on waiting.

'I thought you were a good boy!'

She was genuine desperate.

'Besides, you have not been well.'

Just that moment we stopped by the hotel. I got out and Alia followed leaving aunts in the cab. We went up the desk for my key. I reckoned she was following me up the room.

'Sir!' goes the desk wallah.

'Yeah mate?'

'There was call from your missis.'

'Missis?'

'She said I must tell you it was your missis.'

'She give a name mate?'

'Only missis. Is a kind of wife?'

Noreen knew how to throw a passion killer.

'What she want mate?'

'She say you are to ring her straight away sir. And she hopes you are being good boy.'

'Thank you mister.'

Alia smirking. Then cackling. Then I had to cackle in the bargain.

89

'That Noreen,' I goes.

'You have a fine girlfriend,' she went.

'And you got the hots for a fine fucking geezer,' I turned round and said.

'I hope he is not married.'

'He's married then you got a problem,' I goes. 'What to do with that itch situation. Never forget who your friends are you got a problem Alia. Always ready for helping out you know that.'

'I absolutely will not answer that Nicky,' she goes smiling.

I reckoned she was serious itchy.

When I was up in my room I turned on the TV. Cricket on one channel Urdu on the rest. I belled room service for a cup of tea. Left the TV on. Considered my options. No doubting what I got to do. I got ready for calling up Abdul Hafeez with the number their inspector passed me.

Sitting down as comfortable as it got these days. Which was never very comfortable. Too much passed through the sitting area.

The dog and bone rang before I touched it.

Noreen? She got a track on me?

I picked it up. 'All right my little darlin'?' I went. She was a piece of sweetness you got to say. Most desirous body in the whole of El7. 'You missing me then or what my darlin'? Noreen?'

'Abdul Hafeez,' he went.

'Jesus Christ,' I went.

'No Jesus Christ. This is Muslim country. You are Mr Nicky Burkett?'

'True as I'm stood here.'

'I believe you are given my name.'

'Straight up Abdul. Got your number.'

'You meet me tomorrow.'

'Yeah?'

'In front of your hotel my men will collect you. Eight o'clock in morning.'

'Innit?'

'Motor car will stop. BMW. Three of my men inside. Driver wear green.'

'How you reckon I know this is you Abdul? How I know it ain't some other geezer making out he's my main man?'

'You take my word.'

'Yeah right.'

Bit of a pause while we both reckoned this was too stupid for even considering. Then he started up again.

'You ring number inspector gave you. Check it out.'

'No problem feller.'

I put the Alexander down. Picked it up again and dialled.

'Jesus Christ,' went Abdul.

Geezer with a sense of humour.

'Clock you tomorrow Abdul,' I goes. He grunted. Got a deep grunt.

We were getting serious here.

Question was if I brought old Imran and his CPLC in the game or I kept stum.

I thought about it heavy. Sipped my tea. Knew there was only one way. You got to play both sides.

Like I told the inspector there was official and there was unofficial. You got to have official. Only when you needed a result quick you got to have unofficial in the bargain.

I needed all my mince pies open in the morning. I got ready for turning in only first I belled Noreen.

Back home in Howard Rd she was racing.

'Nicky where it is you keep that garlic, you hear me? Can't bleedin' find anything in this place and would you believe I found some dirty socks of yours, you reckon I'm the kind of woman washes a man's socks or what? I hope you is looking after Alia good Nicky, she emailed me at work gave me your number 'cos you never belled me course and that, Nicky you being a good boy polite not causing no trouble and I hope you two found her brother yet or what, and Nicky you remembering to take them malaria pills I don't want to be catching no malaria off you when you come home, you hear what I'm saying?'

'I got the serious trots Noreen.'

'You got the serious trots Nicky?'

'Serious.'

'Don't you be bringing them back here Nicky I want you proper bunged up and regular when you come back here man.'

'Getting better now Noreen. Poke you one just now.'

'Not while you got them trots Nicky thank you.'

'Noreen I'm telling you they hardly trotting now at all.' Never did listen up what I turned round and said except when it was suiting her. 'Give you a proper touch on this bed right now Noreen, turn you round like a top you hear what I'm saying?'

'Be a new one that Nicky I reckon that sun got to your brain man, like a top you say? You ain't found no little Muslim bird then?' She giggled. 'You got to be bursting by now innit? All them days and no nookie?'

'Got a couple of marriage offers Noreen. And Alia keeps coming across only I turn her down course.' Touch of bluffs good policy.

'Yeah right. Dream on Nicky.'

One thing you got to notice about women. Generally they were brighter than geezers, all excepting in one area. They never did spot the danger zone round their mates.

Still best keep off the subject. 'Where you now Noreen?' I goes. 'You in the bedroom or what?'

'In the kitchen Nicky just getting my tea.'

'You getting them little feelings Noreen? I could just fancy a gander at them little lovely tits of yours. And a touch round that little belly. You getting them feelings Noreen?'

'Mmm … maybe …'

'Get back home and you take a week off work and we get at it like pigeons Noreen, you hear what I'm saying?'

'You never last Nicky. Fall asleep same as usual after a couple of goes.'

'Not this time Noreen. Stay up a fortnight. Right up. Never come down.'

'Chance'd be a fine thing. Nicky you found Kamran yet?'

'No we ain't. I going to see a brigand first thing tomorrow though. Got a gang they reckon. Reckon he put us on the lines.'

'You bell me again Nicky you hear? You keep me dated? Don't just be pissing off up Pakistan and not leaving no messages?'

'Noreen you was sending me up Pakistan, remember? Minding my business keeping it sweet, next stop Pakistan?'

'Yeah well. You be keeping me informed. Daily news.'

I reckoned she was missing me.

'You missing me Noreen or what?' I went.

'Don't you be thinking you so special Nicky.'

'You missing me?'

'Well …'

She was something para was Noreen.

CHAPTER FOURTEEN

ABDUL HAFEEZ WAS a mean geezer and he got a very big moustache.

He was doing the crossword and playing with his pistol. We were in his gaff outside the city, kind of a castle. Crossword was in English. He was swearing in Urdu. Least he was swearing or saying some vicious prayers. Four geezers sitting round looking cool. His boys.

'Three letters!' Abdul went sudden. 'House of pig. Must be pen. Am I right? Am I not right? But it does not fit with three down!'

Nobody moved.

'It is bloody conspiracy! Three letters house of pig it must be pen!'

Young geezer across the way started yacking in Urdu. Then he went in English 'Sty. It is sty.'

Abdul shot him in the foot.

No two ways about it Abdul got a serious attitude.

The young geezer started rolling about. Abdul gave me the smile.

'You are Mr Nicky Burkett?'

'Yeah Mr Abdul. Less you want me to be anyone else that is.'

'You are familiar with the *Times* crossword?'

'Course. All my mates does the fucking *Times* crossword. Stands to reason innit?'

'You are English. We do not have pigs here. Do you think it is pen or do you think it is sty?'

'Run that clue by me again, Mr Abdul?'

'Three letters. House of pig.'

I gave it thinking. Weighed up all the possibilities. Scratched my nozzle.

'Abdul mate I got to make you right. Pen. Never no other fucking thing. House of pig. Pen. End of story.'

'Thank you Mr Nicky. You are clearly a man of wisdom. Now you will have tea.'

'Now you come to mention it, I reckon I will.'

We sat back in our chairs and half a dozen servants went off for giving the news to half a dozen more servants. We cleaned our nails while we waited. Abdul made polite chat to his guest.

'Do you prefer a pistol or a rifle?' he asked conversational.

'Tell you the truth,' I went, 'I ain't fussy. Depends what you want it for I reckon.'

'That is true. Pistol is best for robberies and carjackings. Very good for close-in work. Rifles I find though are best for shooting politicians.'

'True words mate.'

'It is not always easy to get close to politicians except my own politicians. So my men have to pick off the opposition politicians you know from a distance. Tell me Mr Nicky, are you shooting many politicians in England?'

'Not enough Abdul mate, not near enough. Now you mention it we ought to take it more serious.'

'So you have other ways? Poison you are using or the dagger? Or perhaps the bribery is so successful that you are having no need of political murder?'

95

'Reckon it that Abdul. Jobs for the boys innit? Give 'em some easy number and they do what you bleeding want.'

'Perhaps I should think of that. My lawyers advise me that in order to become very big player I must go legit. Do you understand this word legit?'

'Funny you should turn round and mention that Mr Abdul. Noreen my bird she tells me exact the same fucking thing. I come out of nick happy as Larry, then she goes how I want to put it up her I got to stop thieving. So I gives it thinking, weighs it up this way and that way, gives it more thinking, eventual I settles for Noreen. Something about getting old it got to be, know what I mean?'

'Exactly. And they say if I want credibility in New York and Monte Carlo I must have a front. Like a casino, you understand?'

'Well, far as Noreen's concerned it got to be front back and sideways. I never thought of no casino. Idea I reckon. Start one up the market.'

'Perhaps you would like to be money laundering for me? We have partnership in England? You put cash in my account in Zurich?'

'Yeah maybe she buy that one Abdul.' Laundry sounded clean enough for Noreen, got to be a straight up bit of work.

They brought their tea. Tea and jalabee this time round only I passed on the jalabee. Tea got the milk and five sugars already in it only I reckoned it best not complaining now me and Abdul were mates. He sucked his tea under his tash.

'Mr Abdul,' I goes.

'Yes my friend.'

'Came to clock you about a bit of business.'

'I know.' He looked kind of sad to finish the chit chat.

'You heard I was after looking up my mate.'

'I heard yes.'

'And I heard you was the business round here.'

'It is true.'

'I heard beside you Jamil Khan Jamal was kind of a minnow.'

'Jamil Khan Jamal?' His mince pies went very big on me. His hooter went red. His lugs started moving up and down. His trigger finger went itchy.

'Jamil Khan Jamal!' All his boys started hiding behind the furniture. 'Jamil Khan Jamal is how you say a minnow! He is a no one! He is bloody PPP! They are all corrupt in PPP!'

'Bleedin' corruption,' I goes. 'Fuckin' everywhere these days.'

'I am MQM! I own MQM!' I reckoned that got to be like MGM. 'We will destroy PPP party and Jamil Khan Jamal!'

'No problem Abdul. I heard them bleedin' PPP they kidnapped my mate Kamran.'

'Kidnap, yes I heard so. Terrible kidnap.'

'Reckon they want a packet of dosh for him, heard his family got loaded in England.'

'Family loaded? Plenty ammo?'

'Er, rich family Abdul.'

'Rich? You think they like to invest in casino?'

'They ain't real rich Abdul. Come from Walthamstow you get my meaning? Only they reckon come from England and they got to be lined. So they want a bagful of paper or they saw a few bits off my mate Kamran.'

'So you want my help.'

'Need your assist Abdul.'

'So how you pay me?'

'Well I heard you never liked old Jamil too much. Reckoned that might be payment, sort out the geezer like.'

'You crazy?'

'Got to be worth a try.'

We both cackled.

'Worth a try,' he goes. 'Yes worth a bloody try. So now you try something else?'

'Take an IOU?'

'No IOUs.'

Bit of a problem here.

'I tell you what I am thinking,' he goes. Like he got it all sorted from the start. 'I tell you what I am thinking. You see, you can help me with a situation in Ilford.'

'Ilford?' I goes.

'Yes Ilford.'

Oh dear oh fucking me.

'Ilford?' I goes again.

'You hear of this Ilford?'

'Catch a fucking 123. You sure it the same Ilford, Abdul?'

'It is place with outlets.'

'Not sure I catch your drift Abdul. Kind of outlets?'

'Kind of outlets for businessman like Jamil Khan Jamal. Outlets for his merchandise. Shops, businesses, politicians, you understand me?'

'Beginning to understand you. Old Jamil he's a drug baron?'

'Of course.'

'And he retails up Ilford? Goes there himself?'

'Exactly. To keep an eye on business. Twice a year he visits. For two weeks.'

'And you're wanting me for running some kind of errand Abdul? Make his life awkward or what?'

He started cackling again. He got a cackle rumbling like a shark. 'Yes,' he goes. 'Run some errand. Make his life awkward. Yes.' He dabbed his beadies.

'I want you to shoot him,' he goes.

Oh dear oh fucking me.

'Settle his hash.'

We sipped our tea.

'Mr Abdul …' I goes.

'So we understand each other.'

'Understand you any road Abdul. Not too sure you understand me.'

'Very good.'

'I ain't saying I ain't your friend …'

'And if you do not succeed in shooting him …'

'Only I was like trying to give up …'

'There will be problem …'

'Sort of killing geezers …'

'Because I shall inform Jamil Khan Jamal that you are trying to kill him.'

'Noreen don't allow it.'

'And if that fails I shall come over to England and shoot you myself.'

'Thank you Abdul. Reckon I'm understanding your thinking now.'

'With a pistol. SMG.'

'I ain't too worried what sort you use Abdul.'

'Very happy that is all cleared up. Now you are my guest. Tomorrow we go to work. But now the afternoon and evening are ahead of us. Perhaps you like little rest, then we make idle chatter about life.'

My teeth were chattering. Rest might follow later.

CHAPTER FIFTEEN

'YOU SEE,' GOES Abdul, 'we have many problems in Pakistan.'

We sat there on his verandah, one of his boys spraying us with mosquito-hit.

'Yeah?' I goes.

'Once upon time life was settled. All people knew where they were.'

'Hear what you're saying.'

'You were at top or you were at bottom. No buggering about in middle.'

'Right.'

'Now everyone wants to be in middle. All driving rickshaw with motor, no one wanting to pull by hand any more.'

'Yeah.'

'Old trades are dying out.'

'Catch your vibe Abdul.'

'And traditional farming.'

'Yeah?'

'No one grows organic opium any more. All using artificial fertilisers. So quality is terrible.'

'Bleeding disgrace.'

'And nobody learning to assassinate properly.'

'Nah!'

'In my day you were trained from cradle. Now they start when they are grown-up and expect to do it straight away! Result? Botched job, and you have to find craftsman somewhere for patching up.'

'No fuckin' standards innit?'

'And this kidnapping for example.'

'Yeah?'

'Not what it used to be. Very sad.'

'Got to be.'

'Problem here is government.'

'Always the bleedin' same.'

'One year, two years ago, still real industry. One or two kidnappings every bloody week. But then they got CPLC.'

'I heard tell.'

'They have computers. Track you down. Round you up. Then they nobble government so you cannot get away.'

'Nah.'

'Yes! You have heard about direct government?'

'Got the whisper.'

'They take all power from provincial government. It is not democratic.'

'Bleedin' scandalous.'

'When there is no power there is nobody to bribe. So police do not let criminals go.'

'Ain't getting no better.'

'And if criminals thinking they are not being letting go, they do not commit crimes when I tell them!'

'Meaning …'

'Complete breakdown of law and order. No cars hijacked no house robberies no kidnapping. There will be much hardship. I may be forced to make staff redundant.'

'We got that back home.'

'Trouble with Pakistan is everyone got MA Economics. I got MA Economics. He got MA Economics' – pointing up our mosquito-sprayer – 'every one of my boys got MA Economics. But are they knowing how to bribe politicians?'

'Hear what you're saying Abdul.'

'Do they buggery. So bribery becomes another lost art. And I see what comes, we have to shoot whole bloody lot. Needless loss of life among political classes.'

'That bad?'

'Or all my men are made redundant I say again.'

'We got to do something Abdul or geezers be starving.'

'And their children.' He looked likely for weeping.

'And their wives.'

'Never mind their bloody wives.'

'Now you see,' he carries on, 'why it is we are having to diversify, going in other trades.'

'Reckon.'

'It is not our wish being drug barons you understand? We are forcing into it.'

'Catch your drift.'

'We are boxed into corner. What can we do? Make it worse, all sorts come over border from Afganistan due to situation there. Drug sellers, gun merchants, ragamuffins. Opium no longer comes over pass, so they grow it all in Pakistan near frontier. And then they put temptation in our way.'

'Just what happen to me Abdul. Right in my bleeding way all the time. Temptation.'

'They put bloody temptation in way. They say "you can be drug baron". Just when we are forcing to let staff go unless new opportunities come along. So what are we supposed to be doing?'

'No choice innit?'

'No choice at all. We make plenty money. Drugs come down from frontier to Karachi. We buy them. We arrange shipping. We put them in ship. We sell them to middleman. We invest profit in Zurich. No problem.'

'No problem feller.'

'Except that there is rival …'

'Saw it coming.'

'There is bloody buggering Jamil Khan Jamal!'

'Him again! Bleeding spoilsport!'

'And he is bloody drug trafficker from birth! He is not natural employer trying to keep men in work. He is drug baron gangster and he has no breeding!'

'Breeding important innit?'

'Cheap crook. First he tries to find place for himself in street crime. Then he has problem with direct government so he steps over line into drugs. Then he goes back to kidnap!'

'Treading on a few toes am I right?'

'Treading on my bloody bollocks. He must be stopped.'

'Starting tomorrow. Make you right.'

'Tomorrow we will do public service. We rescue your brother cousin young man from England. We stop terrible crime. We save good from evil. Then Jamil Khan Jamal we settle his hash.'

'Reckon you knows your way round the beanfield Abdul. Got your action plan sorted.'

'Inshallah.'

'Salaam mate. Bonjour.'

'And if Jamil Khan Jamal himself gets away tomorrow you shoot him in Ilford.'

'Inshallah.'

Only I kept my fingers crossed while that one, hoped nobody never minded.

CHAPTER SIXTEEN

WE CAME IN fucking army trucks.

Half of Abdul's geezers deserted from the army. When they had it on their toes they took their trucks. And a few other bits.

Four o'clock in the morning they brought us tea. Shook me on the judge and gave me a mug. Manchester fucking United mug. Tea was black and sweet. I got off my mattress and went off for the bathroom. Got a shower came out of the ceiling no expense spared. Get cleaned up for battle.

Four thirty we were on the road.

Two jeeps, six geezers in each. Then two trucks, eight geezers in each. All in camouflage gear. State of the fucking monte. Berets. Boots for kicking. Knives for gouging. Rifles for blowing holes.

And the boys were carrying grenades round their belts. And Jesus they got a mortar like you clocked on the news.

This was very serious agg.

We went cross country round tracks. No tarmac. We left Abdul's gaff cruising. He was in the head jeep. Went past fields of wheat and grass and maize. Cattle in the headlights standing around thin. We went over their plain forty minutes then we started up small hills. Dry. It started getting light very faint showing on the hills.

We went on fifteen minutes.

Then they got ready.

I was sat down the back of a truck. Geezers sitting up nervy. Spitting. Opposite me some young dude getting his blade loose in its holder. He got a serious viz on. Another geezer pissing out the back so he never wet himself in battle. All checking their rifles adjusting their bullet belts.

They gave me a pistol. Reckoned I knew how to use it. Me I was more interested hiding under the truck till later.

We were slowing. Engines. Five thirty the enemy likely for getting up making their tea. Least the servants.

Stopped.

Bunch of trees ahead and inside it they got a big house. Nobody showing yet. Our boys turned the trucks round for a getaway. Driver stayed in each. Rest of us jumped down.

I clocked them all for some big fucker to hide behind. Problem was they were all midgier than me.

Abdul turned and gave me the wink.

'This is life eh?' he goes.

'Yerk,' I goes. Best I could manage. Reckoned when the geezer pissed off the truck I should have taken a quick pony. Before I spoiled my strides. All my trot pills felt like not very useful now.

Hundred metres off the gaff in the trees.

They set up their mortar. Our geezers moved forward getting their grenades out.

'Fire!' hissed Abdul.

Fired the mortar. Fucking fuck.

Mortar missed. In a fucking field.

'Fuck!' goes Abdul. 'Fucking fucking fucking!' Some words you got to turn round and say in English. No words in Urdu for it. Fuck and fire. 'Fucking fire!' he yelled out.

They wound up and fired again.

It went in the top of the building. Same time the boys got close enough for chucking their grenades.

It was like fireworks night in Walthamstow behind the Town Hall. Except I never heard any noise in Walthamstow like the geezer made when he came running out the front door his left arm missing at the shoulder.

I heaved up. Hoped no one noticed.

Then they went in.

They went firing all over the shop. They never gave a toss where they fired. They chucked more grenades then they did some shooting then they went in the doors and windows. Special gaff they got glass in the windows. Abdul's boys never paid mind to glass. Few scratches. They were on a roll.

Then there was firing back. Some of it out of the main house some out of the sheds.

I was on the ground under a fence observing.

Geezer standing by me was the geezer Abdul shot in the foot yesterday. Now it turned out getting shot in the foot was a result. Today he got shot in the brain. He started running, limping. Then he stopped. Bits of him came out the back of his skull.

Jesus fucking Christ.

There was a lot of din. Shouting. Screaming. Fighting going down in doorways. I looked up and clocked one of Abdul's geezers put a sticker right through some poor bastard's gut.

This was never what the geezer from the CPLC meant by helping society.

'Come!' went Abdul sudden at me from out the house.

My legs never wanted to stand up.

'Come!' he screamed.

I went.

It was quieter. Kind of a lull. Reckoned we drove them out the back a moment. Be coming again. Abdul dragged me in the front door.

'This is your man?' he went.

I clocked past three bodies. Young thin geezer quivering alive in the corner.

'All right Kamran?' I goes.

He stared.

'This is your early morning call,' I goes. 'You awake now Kamran? Never falling back asleep again?'

He stared.

'Nicky Burkett?' he goes.

'Who the fuck you think?'

'Nicky Burkett?' he goes again.

'You just turned round and said that Kamran. Getting boring. Now we be getting the fuck out of here, you hear what I'm saying?'

'Nicky Burkett?' he goes again.

'Jesus Kamran.'

'This is your man?' goes Abdul.

'That him yeah.'

'Go!' he shouts.

'Go Kamran!' I shout.

Kamran in a lather. He looked kind of pale. He got a bit of bandage on his left lug. Then I clocked his finger. He got a bit of bandage on that in the bargain.

So they already sent the next package.

Still it was near the end the finger. Never grow back on only it could be worse.

I yanked him out. Running dragged him down the track. He tried the running only he was like a granny after a bus. We were pulling out fast so they all grabbed a bit of him and lifted him in the truck.

Then we were all in.

Then we were gone.

CHAPTER SEVENTEEN

'NICKY!' YELLS ALIA down the Alexander. 'Where have you been? Kamran is back!'

'Yeah?' I goes. I was taking my eleven o'clock siesta up the hotel. After World War Three I got battle fatigue. I was hiding under my pillow dreaming I was up Walthamstow marshes shagging a teenager. Or down West Ham giving the Scousers a hiding. Or round Jimmy Foley's with a can and some whizz.

And I was never scared shitless neither. Trotsky came back with a late plunge.

'Nicky!' yells Alia again. 'You were gone all night! Are you alive? We thought you were kidnapped too! Kamran is back!'

'Got a bad case of the Gandhis,' I goes. 'Sleeping it off heavy.'

'He came here this morning! His finger has been cut off!'

'Only the top half,' I goes.

'What?'

'Er, reckon they only got to slice the top bit innit? Stands to reason, know what I mean?'

'Nicky …'

She was a suspicious bird that Alia.

'Nicky …'

'You want to come up here again and do a spot of nursing Alia? Help me keep my hand in like? Get the old raitha flowing?'

Did the trick that. Got her off the thought path.

'Nicky I do not want to hear any more of your familiar talk thank you. Now we shall come and collect you and you can please come round here and share the celebrations. Please. It will be wonderful to have you here.'

Strange thing I noticed about birds. Start out you were the chief. Couple of weeks and a few curries, there they all were, boss woman. Never knew how it happened, like high tide or eclipse. Natural phenomenon.

'We shall come for you in twenty minutes Nicky.'

'Ten four Alia.' I went off for the bathroom.

Alia's family took me in their front room. Last time I was there it was wailing and blubbing. This time they got the fruit juices out for a jump-up.

'Nicky!' they all went. 'Kamran is back!'

Most of him was back as it goes. Still no point splitting hairs over a bit got left behind.

'We must thank you very much!'

They sussed it?

'If you had not gone to Lahore and begun whole process we would not know where he was.' Uncle talking. 'Then CPLC involved and immediately Jamil Khan Jamal returned Kamran. It is wonderful.'

'Innit?' I goes.

'We feared that our hospitality would be questioned for ever.'

'No problem Uncle.'

'He is fit in mind and body.'

'Mostly.'

'Yes … mostly. He is fine young man.'

110

'Straight up geezer is Kamran.'

Kamran came out the back. He looked ripe for pegging it.

'Kamran you looking sharp geezer. Look like you might last the week, long as the wind stays right.'

'Nicky I feeling like shit.'

'Kind of how you look feller. How's the old fingers eh? Nine out of ten?'

He sort of shuddered.

'And that fifth gear? Still got a bit left for them birds to nibble on?'

'Nicky no bird never want to clock me again I'm telling you, yeah?'

'Don't be so hard on yourself Kamran. Plenty of birds got a thing going for geezers missing a few bits. Ain't your clit finger I hope?'

He started off cackling then. Fortunate only Alia heard and she never understood or she was keeping stum about it.

'Nicky you going to tell me what the fuck going down here, yeah?'

'Some other time mate.'

'My family they all reckon how this CPLC got it fixed.'

'Good fucking geezers Kamran. Old Imran there, fucking dog's bollocks.'

'They never got me out!'

'Keep it down Kamran. You never whistled?'

'Nah. You told me button it.'

'Good man. They maybe reckon there was just a touch of the illegals. Anyhow that Jamil, never want him knowing how I was too involved.'

'I think he knows Nicky. I heard your boss man, he say he told him.'

'Shit. I never credited it for real. He stitched me.'

'Like a fucking truss Nicky. His price.'
'Shit.'

* * *

Alia got the shopping lurgy bad. She got feverish. Her and me and a few cousins went round Karachi like they got the last market stalls left on earth. She was buying presents for back home.

Me I reckoned Green St down East Ham was the same difference except Green St got Upton Park down the bottom. Alia never agreed.

She got dresses and material and jewellery and pictures and a basket of cashews. Then she got more dresses. And more material. Then she got a carpet.

''Scuse me Alia,' I turned round and said.

'Yes Nicky?'

'You sending that carpet freight or what?'

'No Nicky.'

'How you getting that back up Walthamstow you mind my asking?'

'Wait and see Nicky.'

I got a funny feeling round that carpet. Alia already emptied out her cases giving out all the chocolates and sweets and biscuits from England round her family. She was ready for putting the dresses and material there. Only her cases never fitted a bleeding carpet.

I packed my bag round the hotel and they collected me. Alia packed all her bags by her family and they took them up the airport in a couple of trucks. Carpet they got in the boot of our motor.

We got out the motor. We went up departures. Cousins carrying the carpet. And the cases. Then they went home after an hour or so of kissing and hugging.

It was me and Alia on our tod just like we started. She was leaking emotional. I was thinking on the carpet.

She was still waving even after they all disappeared out the back and went home drinking chai. 'Oh Nicky,' she went. 'It is so terrible. When I am in England I want to be in Pakistan. When I am in Pakistan I want to be in England. Oh oh dear.'

Behind the counter was a tasty bird, gave me the smile.

'I think you have to pay excess,' the bird turned round and said in English. To Alia.

'It is my friend's hand baggage,' went Alia, sudden not distressed at all.

'Hand baggage ...' I went weak.

Then before I went anywhere I was rolling out that carpet on their floor taking a fucking good butcher's on it. Hardly likely Alia got a stash in there only half the merchants up the market knew how we were taking it back up Walthamstow and maybe wanted to include a message. Never fancied doing my time up some nick in Karachi.

It was clean.

'Hand baggage ...' I went weak trying it with Alia again. 'I ain't got no hand baggage Alia. I got some book about cricket your uncle gave me for helping with the dozing. Then I ain't got nothing.'

'Exactly. You see I could not take it because I already have two cases as hand baggage. I am really only allowed one bag. This carpet will be like your bag.'

She done me up like a kipper.

When they checked my ticket and all the business I picked up her carpet. It tucked nicely under one arm except the arm nearly fell off.

'We going to fall out the sky Alia. Plane ain't nearly strong enough. Anyhow I never climb up that ramp.'

113

'You could always put it on your head Nicky like they do in Pakistan,' she went. Getting her rocks off giggling.

I hauled it up their departure lounge. Round their duty free. Round their canteen. Up their gate then in their bus to the plane then up their steps. I got in there right quick, shoved past all the old biddies trying to get up the luggage cupboards. Only problem was the old biddies fought back, all carrying a dozen cases and wanting a bit of space. We bashed each other plenty only I got my carpet in there. Took up a whole luggage compartment.

Then I relaxed.

We were leaving Pakistan. Soon be back in Walthamstow.

I got my cricket book and took forty winks straight off. Woke up every time they put a meal down then read the cricket book and went back dozing. Woke up for changing planes up the Gulf. Bought a dozen personal stereos for retailing round the snooker halls. Bought some dates for my mum keep her sweet.

When we got near London I remembered there was something I forgot.

'Alia,' I goes, 'you want to join that club then babe before it get too late?'

'What club Nicky?'

'Mile high club course Alia, you up for that?'

'Mile high club Nicky?'

'Know what that is my darlin'? Want me to show you?'

'Just tell me Nicky I think is safer.'

'Touch of the other up the toilet innit? Least it don't have to be up the toilet depending. Very exclusive club Alia. Bit of howsyourfather one mile up in the sky. Seeing as how I got shot of them trots now, like a better proposition all round, you want to have that bit you promised back up Karachi? Or maybe just a feel round?'

'Nicky! I never promised anything you terrible man. Just think of Noreen. She is my friend.'

'My friend too Alia.'

'And anyway you know I could never do anything like that. It is all right for white girls.'

'Noreen ain't very white.'

'And for black girls but not for Asian girls as you well know.'

'Never even a little cuddle?'

I reckoned she was wavering again.

'Excuse me sir could I just put your tray down, here is your breakfast.'

Shit. They ruined another beautiful friendship. Always bringing you grub on their planes stopping you even getting started.

Not long after we were back in London.

PART TWO

BACK AGAIN

CHAPTER EIGHTEEN

'Nicky!'
      'Noreen you little darlin'.'

There she was waving at me soon as I came out of Arrivals. Bleeding brilliant bird Noreen you got to credit her. Bits and bobs in all the right places, loved me in the night like I was Mr Big, Noreen was one Al bit of stuff.

'Nicky!'

'Noreen how you managed without me then eh?'

We gave it that in the middle of Arrivals. Felt her little bits boring into me like they were digging for Australia. Curled her knee round me like I was putting it up her there and then no messing.

'Alia! I hope he done everything you wanted and minded his manners innit?'

'He has been a very good boy Noreen.'

Little beauty that Alia.

'And we found Kamran you know.'

'What you said in your e-mail. Bleedin' great eh? He in one piece?'

'Nearly,' I goes.

'Nearly?'

'Nicky,' goes Alia, 'we will talk about all this later. Kamran is coming on the next plane. Here come my family now.'

Mum and dad and uncles and aunties and sisters and brothers and cousins and maybe a few she never recognised came along for the ride. They fell on her like she was a special dinner.

Noreen came up Thiefrow in the minivan they got Alia's family. We all got in no problem then Alia's luggage shoved it two feet down on its axle. Noreen and me we got down the back for a little hug up, only nothing too good on account of all the spectators being Asian.

'Nicky you ain't been losing a few pounds? All them curries and you got thin?'

'Touch of the bowel problems Noreen. Spot of the lurgy. Quality toilet time.'

'You poor boy.' Noreen reckoned I was a poor boy about once in five years. Rest of the time she gave me heavy brain agg. Best to take advantage when it came. 'You poor boy. You can cook me a very nice meal when we get home. I bet you are dying to get back to a bit of home cooking.'

'You got the shopping?'

'Good breadfruit on the market this week Nicky so my mum reckons. Stop on our way home. You cook them up nice in the oven, you know, and you make a bit of stew with it.'

'Reckon that jetlag just kicked in Noreen. Serious time zone problem. Only cook breakfast this time of day.'

'Hope that jetlag ain't too bad Nicky, hoping you could manage a bit of loving before it strike you down.'

'Try to make exceptions then. Got to be early morning style loving though. What way we normally do it early mornings?'

'Well last time I remember Nicky there was something about a cup of tea involved after I took a mouthful and then ...'

'Oh yeah ...'

We were both giggling like Geordies.

'Then after that them breadfruit Nicky.'

Surprising Noreen never wasted away while I was up Pakistan, what with no geezer to cook nor for a spot of good loving.

She was over me like she was tasting me up. Soft little mouth breathing and blowing and kissing and smoothing over everywhere gave me the serious shaking, made me gasp and pant out loud.

'Christ Noreen.'

She laid me back and she moved her tits up my gob then she moved down so they were round my legs and she was touching heavy down on my bare essentials. Next time she kissed me on the gob her legs were over me and she was serious.

Been there three hours and no tales about jetlag got a listening from her. We already did it twice and now she had to be getting on top on account of I was flatter than a pancake, all except in one area got a life of its own.

'Yes Nicky,' she went hissing soft and breathy when she took me in her easy. She moved back and forward and she clocked down on my mug and she started laughing, cackling like a fairy and she went 'oh yes Nicky' while she moved again and then she started shuddering all over and soft little cries came from far back and she went on till I was joining her there, only I was hardly worth a spurt. I was wasted.

Birds. I never knew a bird like Noreen, truth to tell. Got to be her being so bleeding clever at school and that, I always heard how the clever ones were the worst ones.

'Oh Nicky that was a good one.'

'Oh …' I went. Then I was sleeping. She was still on me. She was never there next morning so some time in the night she took herself off.

And next morning started early.

* * *

First off I woke up giving it thinking.

Plenty of time for thinking on account of I was still on Pakistan time, woke up middle of the Walthamstow night wanting half a dozen hard-boiled eggs for breakfast. So I started up on all the bits never fitted and likely for giving out major aggravation.

How I saw it there were a few problems.

Kamran disappeared up Pakistan. Alia and Noreen got me looking for him. No other fucker supposed to know anything about it. Still I got jumped in Walthamstow by half a dozen kids trying for warning me off.

Then I got another word up Karachi airport. Old Bill told me to fuck off out.

So some fucker back home did know Kamran was going and did know I was going after. Fact was they lined up Kamran. Got to be. Thousands of geezers went up Pakistan. Three main reasons for it. Either visiting family or coming off the brown or getting hitched up. Often all three the same time, you clocked your granny and did your clucking and had your wedding all in a fortnight. But nobody kidnapped these geezers. Kamran though he got kidnapped. Maybe it was like we turned round and said, they reckoned his family was pigging it. More likely though it was on account of his city number. Him working for some money firm up west. Money firm equals money.

Then there was another bit. Jamil Khan Jamal got an interest in Ilford. Maybe he was the man. Maybe he was the geezer got the bit of work sorted, then he was the geezer went and did it, then he lined up the paperwork after. Wholesale, retail and fence all in one hit.

So they stitched Kamran up before he went and then they gave me the warning off a bit of protection. Then they were following Kamran then they were following Alia and then they were following the whole fucking lot of us.

I reckoned though they got one problem they never even knew about, all the way through. How they saw it, some big money firm up the City was likely to give a toss about their Asian kid out of Walthamstow just on account of he worked for them a couple years. They got an understanding reality problem here.

Always dangerous some tosser never knew the score. Like here they started cutting bits off Kamran and reckoned that meant his bosses gave them a sackful of dosh. They reckoned it like this, so they were hardly likely for stopping when they got one minor hitch. They were likely for being dangerous.

I went back over it all from the start. Jamil Khan Jamal was after big spends off Kamran's bosses for his ransom. It never panned out. Jamil Khan Jamal came back to his business in Ilford. He was planning for being fucked off with me and Alia. Case it slipped his mind, Abdul Hafeez happened to mention his problems were all down to me, and in the bargain I was after whacking him.

Jamil Khan Jamal might want to be sorting my lifestyle.

CHAPTER NINETEEN

THE WINDOWS CRASHED in.

Four o'clock in the morning I was making tea. Done my thinking. Head like a dishcloth.

One thing though, least I was making a proper cup of rosie in my own gaff in my own borough. Proper tea. They never knew about making tea up Pakistan. I was happy enough.

Kitchen was out the back by the bedroom. Front room was at the front. Bathroom next to it.

All the windows came in from the front. They took them out with shooters.

Four o'clock in the morning some fuckers were shooting out my fucking windows. It was never reasonable behaviour.

Thank fuck Noreen was out the back. I went down the floor, reckoned first off it was bricks, crawled in the front room for the SP on the situation. No bricks in the room. Things that came in the windows were things that kept on coming and stuck in the ceiling.

I got on the blower to the Old Bill. Turned out they got thirteen calls in five minutes on the subject, ten of them off me.

'Noreen,' I goes, 'off the bed down the fucking floor.'

'Wh'appen?'

'Fuck knows. Fuckers shooting out our windows.'

'Jesus.'

'Only the front. I belled Old Bill. I got the bolt on. Made a cup of tea you want one.'

'Later Nicky. Who the fuck is shooting us?'

'Fuck knows. Pakistan geezers I reckon. Fuck knows.'

Sirens started off. Old Bill never be arsed on a straight up robbing, turn up half a week after. Shooting though they loved a good shooting. Even middle of the night they shifted their bollocks for a good shooting. Four motors in six minutes and they sealed the street off in ten. Made some noise. Just what you wanted to keep the neighbours happy.

Forensics all over the shop. They even dabbed for fingerprints, lot of bleeding use and left smudges on the walls. Couple of windows were shattered all over, others the shots went straight through leaving little holes. They dug them out the walls and ceiling. Rifle bullets.

Rifles in Walthamstow?

Shotguns yeah no problem, even plenty handguns these days only never rifles. Any doubting previous it was Pakistan geezers, it got cleared up now.

And in the bargain they were threatening my woman.

Old Bill asked some questions. Me and Noreen we never got time for conferring so I never knew what to turn round and say. I tried out the state of shock leaving me speechless.

'We reckon it might be geezers from Pakistan,' went Noreen.

'Oh yeah?' went PC Burns. Blonde bird big tits. We met once before and Noreen got extreme leery. Never pleased to see PC Burns middle of the night or any other time.

'Oh yeah?' went some tosser off the firearms squad turned up looking husky. 'Got in some war up the North West Frontier no doubt?'

'Nah, down by Karachi matter of fact,' I went. Should have kept my gob shut.

'What you want to tell us Nicky?' goes DS O'Malley out of Chingford. 'What you reckon this is about? You got enemies or are you telling us this is mistaken identity or what? You been treading on any toes in some drug war? You got up someone's nostrils and this is a warning? Best you tell us now, eh?'

I knew DS O'Malley from way back. Fact was he lifted me on a bit of shoplifting when I was a nipper and then a couple of murder charges. He mellowed though, only wanted me on drug charges this time. But he was pig sick all the same, you joined CID to get out of nights and here he was on nights. Not such a bad geezer O'Malley, still he never got my sympathy vote.

'He went up Pakistan,' goes Noreen again. 'We reckon some warlord there followed him back.' She clocked me good. Seemed like the proper action here was telling the truth. Came a bit unfamiliar.

'Some Pakistan geezer reckons I going to waste him,' I goes.

'You? You and whose army? For what?'

'Long story. He got told I was after sending him up the road.'

'Pakistan warlord?' PC Burns was cackling. 'You send him up the road?'

'Up the fucking road. Over the river. Down south London, you get me?'

'We know you did waste a couple Nicky ...' went O'Malley.

'It was an accident,' I goes.

'Only that was then. And it was local. Now is this very likely and ain't it better you tell us the truth from the start or what?'

We just tried the truth and where did it fucking get you.

They stayed the night. One stage we got ten Old Bill in our flat. Another thirty outside. Then they got journalists like moths. We never tried telling them the truth or anything else, only one ever gave any cred was Bridget Tansley off the *Walthamstow Guardian*.

Bridget was one who got away as it happens. When I got in the news accidental a few times she always gave me a good spread, so I reckoned natural that might be good for a touch of the bunk-up. Me and her though our relationship turned out always platonic, mainly on account of I never could get near her. Preferred a good story to a good bunk-up it looked like. No accounting for tastes.

I digress. O'Malley reckoned next morning I got to go up Chingford and make a statement. First off I got to get some kip. I was not happy.

Neighbours were none too happy neither.

And least of all happy was that Noreen. She was not a very pleased bird and I was not king of her castle.

'Nicky you come on back here and what we got? Serious grief is what we got! Be doing my brain in!'

'Noreen eat your muesli up, you going to be late for work.'

'Nicky we know you was very helpful going out to Pakistan like that. And Kamran it sounded like he was well safe. I ain't saying I ain't grateful. Only bringing that trouble back here, you have to do that? We ain't got enough trouble of our own in Walthamstow?'

'Old Bill never believe it got any connection.'

'Old Bill believe what they want. All I know is no one came shooting up my windows previous.'

As it goes they were my windows, seeing as it was my gaff. Not a good plan pointing this out for Noreen just now though.

'Nicky you reckon they were only after shooting up our windows like some warning, or you reckon they were after shooting us?'

Difficult to know what to turn round and say. Always difficult to know how to treat your woman. No doubting how Noreen was a brilliant bird. Still all the same she was a bird. Not like a geezer. Never knew how they might turn.

I gave it brain.

'Nicky I asked you a question innit?'

Best I tell her the Auntie Ruth in the bargain. Other problem with women was some of them were cleverer than geezers, get it out of you anyhow and then you were in shit creek.

'Noreen there was this geezer up Pakistan, he got serious vex now.'

'No surprises there Nicky, I reckon you got to be vex if you go shooting up people's windows.'

'Noreen, like I told Old Bill, he reckon I going to whack him. Serious.'

'Whack him Nicky? Kill him? Whatever you say to him make him think that?'

'I never turned round and said any fucking thing Noreen. I never want to whack the fucking geezer anyhow. Some other geezer told him I was going to stop his fucking clock for him. And him being a warlord. And the other geezer being some other warlord.'

'Jesus Nicky how you meet these people, you just go out for a curry and they sit at your table or what?'

'This geezer Jamil Khan Jamal Noreen …'

'Yeah?'

'Being the geezer kidnapped Kamran.'

'Ah.'

'And this other geezer Imran Khan …'

'I heard of him, cricketer innit?'

'Some other Imran Khan.'

'He related to this Jamil Khan?'

'Noreen you got to let me finish up or I get confused. They got a lot of Khans up Pakistan. This Imran Khan being helpful but not quick enough before Kamran gets bits chopped, we went round this other geezer Abdul Hafeez.'

'Yeah …'

'Some other warlord. He like helped get old Kamran back only in the bargain he was telling this Jamil Khan Jamal I was after giving him the big smack.'

'Yeah but why Nicky?'

'On account of Jamil Khan Jamal is his enemy. Taking his business. So he informs Jamil Khan Jamal so Jamil comes after me so I settle his account after all, end of story. How he sees it anyhow. Then old Abdul he got the clear run, yeah?'

'Jesus Nicky.'

'Me in the fucking middle. Fucking sad story innit?' Trying for getting some kind of advantage here.

'Only that was up Pakistan Nicky.'

'Yeah only this Jamil you never credit it he got retails up Ilford.'

'Ilford!'

'Bit of a front job. Wholesalers up Ilford Lane. Do a bit of laundering. Comes over twice a year, tend to his business.'

'And he's here now.'

'And he here now straight after. Reckons I kill him. So he get his bad attitude in first.'

'Try to shoot you.'

'Maybe get in a few frighteners first. Few giggles.'

'Oh Nicky.' She came over and gave me her cuddle. Her cuddle always worked like a jack in the box on me. 'Oh Nicky. Ain't he heard how you're just one big soft pussycat and that?'

'Not too sure about that Noreen. Never want to damage my rep too much you understand.'

'Oh Nicky.' She gave me a pat like a puppy.

Only there was more problem here.

One time back a couple of years, Noreen got sliced on my account. Earhole right down her jaw. Some fucker wanted me warned off. Some high-up Old Bill. Best way he reckoned was do up my bird. So he sliced her. Glad to say in the end he turned out not so alive as he had been up till then. All the same I never could make it up to Noreen. Even though you hardly clocked it now, still I never wanted it coming round again.

'Noreen you reckon you better go round your mum's?'

'Oh Nicky.'

'You reckon it best?'

'Oh I don't know Nicky.'

'I ain't going to be here neither Noreen. Hid up.'

'Nicky you got to go to Old Bill with all this. Some geezer believe you. You find that TT, he got to be an inspector by now, he believe you.'

DS TT Holdsworth, they called him TT on account of his wheels. He got me in more trouble than I ever got myself in. One time he wanted my assist lifting some geezer shafted a copper. Not my problem some copper got shafted. More likely I hung out a flag. Still some reason TT always reckoned I was his mate. Kept on turning up after that, putting some bit of work my way like a contract kill. Just on account of I accidentally totalled a couple of geezers maybe he reckoned I was in it for the laughs.

I thought about it. 'I reckon not Noreen. Just keep under the counter I reckon a couple of weeks.'

'Nicky ...?' She never liked it.

'And you go by your mum's?'

'Maybe …'

She curled up on me. We finished up the night how we started it. Only difference was this time the nookie got air conditioning. She belled her work and took a bit of that flex time.

And Jamil Khan Jamal got one more thing to answer for. Not only he was wanting to put me away permanent. Meanwhile he was stopping me getting a touch of fucking howsyourfather off my bird.

CHAPTER TWENTY

'R AMEEZ,' I WENT on the mobile.

'Nicky Burkett! Nicky fucking Burkett! Nicky fucking Burkett I heard you was up Pakistan poisoning relations am I right? How we was peaceful going about our business my people then you went in starting war! Am I right?'

'Yeah Rameez, minding your business no problem, bit of robbing, bit of kidnapping.'

'Ex-actly my man! My people got to make a living and now life is made so difficult! Anyhow Nicky what the fuck you want? My time is precious as you know. This a social call or what it is?'

First time I knew Rameez he was only one minor league vicious gangster. Now three four years later he was Nation-wide First Division vicious gangster. Got to hand it to him he kept on getting promotion. Now he was after Premiership vicious gangster, get the television dosh.

When he got bored and nothing else to do he was after putting it up our Sharon. Rest of his spare time he drove his Audi round. Then again his driving was his business, making his rounds, doing his slicing.

Me and Rameez we were never what you call mates. He was too fucking terrifying. Before he started fucking my sister we were familiar in a business way. Like I offered a routine bit of work, he charged a fucking big wallop of dosh and then he killed a few geezers. I was never quite in control of the situation.

'Rameez I needs your assist.'

'Of course Nicky I knows you needs my assist. And I am glad to give you my assist. Usual rates it goes without saying.'

'Mates' rates?'

'Usual rates Nicky if you my mate or not.'

'How about special rates on account of you putting it up my sister?'

'You should feel honoured Nicky. Now you tell me what is going down here and I shall perform my task and take my percentage.'

'Rameez things got shady round Pakistan.'

'Yeah?'

'Feller Jamil Khan Jamal came back over here after me. Got a serious attitude problem.'

'Jamil Khan Jamal?'

'Him.'

'Nicky you should tread very softly round Jamil Khan Jamal. He is one very serious person.'

'What I'm telling you Rameez. I needs your assist.'

'Nicky I am thinking you got a problem with Jamil Khan Jamal you should go into hibernation. You know anyone in Iceland Nicky or Poland? Or New Zealand or them Falklands or any other kind of land?'

'Rameez I got thinking you maybe protect me?'

'Protect you Nicky?'

'I believe that's what I just turned round and said Rameez. You being a protection geezer.'

'Nicky I think you maybe do not understand protection. Protection is some geezer start up a club or a cab office, he

133

pay me protection or I smash the fucking place up. Protection is not like I protect you. First you ain't got no percentage for me innit. Second your life ain't like got any value on it. Unless you got life insurance and I get a cut or what?'

'I ain't got life insurance Rameez. I sort of reckoned you help me out. Being as us like old mates you hear what I'm saying?'

'Hah!'

Then we got one long pause.

'Rameez?' I went. 'You still there?'

'Course I'm still here Nicky. I only waiting for you to come up with a more sensible suggestion.'

'I give you all Jamil Khan Jamal's dosh?'

'Yeah?'

'Yeah.'

'And how you get it?'

'You get it for me.'

'Then you give it to me?'

'Yeah.'

Then we got another long pause.

'Nicky you think maybe you got a problem on your logic here?'

'Sounds sweet to me Rameez.'

He knew how there was something had to be wrong in my thinking only he was never too sure what it was.

'Nicky you reckon we meet something, discuss your action plan or what?'

'What I'm after Rameez.'

'I bring Afzal and Aftab. You bring your capo.'

'My capo?'

'Course.'

'That like a hat?'

'Your capo Nicky. Like your counsellor.'

134

Only counsellor I knew was like my probation officer, who I had when I was a villain to help me change my ways. Fine geezer Andy, always good for a cup of rosie and a spot of the old counselling. Changed my ways. Got me cutting out the sugar altogether by the time we finished. Not sure he'd get the same success rate on Rameez though.

'Where you want to meet Rameez? Round my mum's when you putting it up Sharon?'

'Don't be ridiculous Nicky. Sometimes I think you ain't got no fucking cool at all. We have a meeting in like a meeting place, yeah?'

'Fair enough Rameez. No problem, know what I mean?'

'Ambala down Leyton High Rd. You know it?'

'Course.'

'See you there.'

'Right.'

Pause.

'Any special time Rameez or I go down and hang around a few days?'

'Nine thirty.'

'Today?'

'Natural.'

'See you later Rameez.' He was off. Probably have a quick touch up our Sharon first.

I was half way up Noreen again when the bleeding doorbell rang.

'Erk?' I went. 'Fuck!' We came back for getting our things together after Noreen's work. Reckoned we'd get a touch of the other before we hid up. I was just getting into it and she was breathing heavy.

The bell went again.

'You better get the door Nicky,' Noreen turned round and said.

'Who me?'

'Seeing as I'm underneath and I can't get up. Some other position, course I'd be there.' Then she giggled and that set her off on a sort of shudder and all in all I plopped out.

'Fuck,' I turned round and said.

'Later Nicky,' she went.

'You reckon they come to shoot me?'

'Ring the doorbell?'

'Probably them religions like last week.'

It went again.

'Coming!' went Noreen. Then she cackled again. 'Except we didn't,' she goes. 'Nicky you make haste, you hear me?'

I got my strides on and went downstairs.

It was Alia.

'Alia!' I went. 'Favourite bird! Top bit of lovely! You looking good Alia, know what I mean?'

She started trickling.

'Oh Nicky,' she went.

'You ain't happy?'

'Is Noreen there?'

'Just tidying up a bit Alia. You come on in.'

We went upstairs. Noreen in the front room gleaming. Fuck knows how she did it, fully dressed and brushed her curlies and got her blusher on.

'Alia!' she went. 'What the problem sister?'

'It is Kamran,' she went. 'They have kidnapped him. Again.'

136

CHAPTER TWENTY-ONE

ALIA WAS BLUBBING in buckets.

'He lost any more of them digits Alia?' I goes. 'You got any bits through the post and that? Or courier?'

'Nicky!' went Noreen.

'We got a message,' goes Alia.

'Yeah?'

She pulled it out the envelope.

When Jamil Khan Jamal got himself involved there was never any fucking around with words cut out of newspapers. He wrote the thing out. He even signed the fucker.

'One crore pounds sterling ...' it went.

Not very helpful for a lot of people this side the channel. Fortunate Alia's family reckoned how much that was.

'... for Mr Malik. Soon we are removing one more piece.'

Kind of sinister.

'Noreen,' I goes, 'you getting out of here, yeah?'

'Don't reckon they're after me Nicky. Still I catch your drift. You go by your mum's?'

'Jesus Noreen. Sooner get kidnapped.'

'Best you go round and tell her what's going down though, right?'

'You say so.'

'Alia, you told the police yet?'

'Yeah, they're round my mum and dad's now. I just came round to warn you. We are safe from anything further. The whole community has turned out down Queen's Road and no strangers could get in there.'

'Bit late.'

'Yes. They have taken Kamran. But you are not safe here I am thinking.'

'How'd they lift Kamran?'

'They took him from the airport Nicky. They watched him come in and they watched him leave the airport, then they rammed us on the North Circular, shunted our car off the road.'

'Jesus. Took just him?'

'Only him. They left the rest of the family standing there. It seemed they did not want any more of us. Perhaps they will take someone from another family for more money, I don't know.'

'You told his guvnors?'

'They received another letter like this one at his work.' So they tracked him from his job place. Start to finish. They got to be tracing Asians worked in the city. Some of them bound to go up Pakistan once in a while for clocking the family. Pick them up round Karachi in kidnapping season. Put the demands on the family and they get the wedge off the work. Nice.

Normal times they stayed up Pakistan where the shooting and slicing was quality. Only now they came up London on account of we pulled on old Jamil's hooter hairs and he was getting serious vex.

We packed up our toothbrushes and a bit of weed and then we were out of there.

Noreen went by her mum's. When they knocked down Chingford Hall estate they gave her family a proper home.

Now they got a front door and a gate and they even got pizza delivered.

When we were kids Noreen's dad used to take me and Jimmy Foley and Sherry McAllister football playing with her brother Ricky, went to school with us up McEntee. Saturday morning we were in the under-ten league until we got expelled. Unfortunate incident, total misunderstanding. Just cause Whipps Cross Hospital got put on full alert like a train crash, everyone called back from their beds and massage parlours, they reckoned it was down to us and all over a game of football.

I toddled out of Howard Rd up Church Hill across Hoe St and down the market thinking on the old days. Back then when we were nine not a single one of us ever went to prison. We never even nicked a motor.

Mercedes Marty Fisherman was advanced for his age, lifted motors at ten and his first Merc at eleven. Dean Longmore started on pushbikes from five, nicked scooters from seven and a Robin Reliant at eight. When he really got in the swing around thirteen fourteen he used to ride a motor every night before he did his homework. Very conscientious about his homework was Dean. Jimmy Foley was kind of retarded, never learned to drive till he was fourteen nor put it up a bird till he was fifteen and a half. We put it down to allergies.

Noreen's mum and dad were straight though. Never let Ricky play with us after about eight in the morning. Even then he only got to think bad thoughts and his mum came steaming out of Chingford Hall ready for whacking the lot of us with her rolling pin. They ought to put her in uniform and called her Old Bill.

On Hoe St by the Central there were Albanians trying to earn a penny washing windscreens. They were talking

Albanian. Up the market Africans were speaking African. Kurds speaking Kurd. Arabs speaking Arab. Scousers speaking Scouser. Fucking nobody spoke Walthamstow any more.

All trying to make a bob or two. Most of them refugees and all the poor bastards got was vouchers. No real dosh at all. It was simpler to steal the groceries than start exchanging all their vouchers. And you wanted a bus ride you had to hijack the bleeding bus.

Lifting groceries was never difficult anyhow. When we were kids Mum used to send me and Sharon out shopping with a tenner on Saturday mornings or after school. Those days there was a supermarket on Hoe St by the bus stop, so after we spent the dosh down the amusements Sharon stood by the end of the aisle and yelled when security came. After a bit we got known there so we went up Sainsbury's or Kwiksave. Sainsbury's no point yelling, you just grab it and go. Kwiksave half the security was ex-cons anyhow so you only had to tip them a freeman's and you walked.

I carried on up the market kind of sentimental. When they started the new library we used to nick all the books on true crime looking for hints. One time Mum kicked me out I slept round the market and made a quid or two putting up the stalls in the morning. Cheese or banana stalls were the best, doshed me in kind. By the market the flats on top of the shops I generally found somewhere to kip. Half of them were Asian families ran the shops, always give you a meal. Other half above the empty shops were white riff-raff, broke in and started the gas and electricity so they could squat a while. Junkie heaven it was up there, score any time you were clucking.

Then you got thirsty you could always come down and mix with the Tennents crowd. Always someone give you a drink by the post office and a bit of a natter in the bargain. Never troubled you when you didn't answer on account of they were too pissed to make any sense. They carried on sweet.

When we got no need for dosh or we got bored we used to go for a laugh nicking out the Oxfam shop down the far end of the High St.

There was a geezer worked in the Oxfam shop been away himself, three years up Wayland. Worked there some kind of volunteer, part of his parole he reckoned. First time he copped us thieving he very near split himself cackling. 'You're taking the fucking piss aintcha?' he went. 'Making fuckin' joke with me or what? Thieving out of the bleeding Oxfam shop? Fuckin' hell you kids I'll give you the fuckin' things you want them, there ain't nothing here going over 50p. And what the fuck you want with that fuckin' jigsaw anyhow?'

Not the way we clocked it though. Not the way the manager clocked it neither. It was him made the whole thing lively.

He got an obsession. He hated anything nicked out of his gaff. Two pence or twenty notes he was never having it. He wanted villains nicked and he wanted them nicked. End of story.

Gave the game an edge. Some other life he got to have been some major league sprinter.

One time that manager chased Elvis Littlejohn one end the market to the other. Whole mile long the guidebooks reckon, longest street market in Europe made Walthamstow famous. Elvis nicked a packet of ping pong balls, used. Value 20p. Elvis was so nifty those days he could get under the stalls, still that manager chased him knocking away old biddies right and centre trying to buy their dasheen for the weekend. Elvis only got clean away when he fucked off down the Central and took a cab out the borough. Ten years later we still had a cackle whenever we got yacking about it.

Happy fucking days.

I turned right on Palmerston Rd then shanked up and over Forest Rd then up Priory Court where Mum lived.

When they refurbished Priory Court they reckoned they changed the people lived there. Made them legit.

They reckoned how you kept people in shit they went out thieving but you gave them central heating they got jobs up the city selling timeshares. Kind of a pity how I saw it. Kind of bad for your reputation.

They were all there when I got up Mum's. There was Mum and Shithead. There was Kelly visiting and the boy Danny. Then there was our Sharon and her kid. Sharon got her own gaff now, doing all right since she took over radio control on the visiting massage service. Got a mortgage and shopped up Ilford. Still she was back Priory Court half the time, how we all stuck there like shit to a blanket.

'All right Dad?' goes Danny.

'All right mate?' I goes. 'All right Kelly?'

'All right Nicky.'

'Dad what you brought me back from Pakistan?'

'Brought you a Muslim bird mate, all wrapped up nice, that sweet with you?'

'Pull the other one Dad it's got bells on.' Danny seven years old now. Far as I knew he never got his leg over yet.

'Mum I got you some dates and some vodka out of that Gulf.'

'Thank you Nicky. Hope you behaved yourself up Pakistan.'

'Danny I got you something to take to school. Hope that's sweet with you.'

Got him a TV. Four-inch screen. Just the size for taking in classes.

'Wick-ed Dad! Ex-cellent! Dad you are so cool!'

'Spoil the boy,' goes Shithead. 'Make him think money grows on bleeding trees.'

'Why don't you fucking button it,' I goes.

'You got lip coming out your arse,' goes Sharon.

Danny turned on his TV then he went off up the bathroom for a proper butcher's.

'You all right Nicky?' went Kelly. 'No probs up that Pakistan?'

'Nah. All sorted. You still humping that Barry regular?'

'I'm still seeing Barrington if that's what you mean. He treats me good.'

'Lucky you.' Hard to believe Kelly was fucking a German name of Barrington, still no accounting for tastes. 'Mum, you got any tea or you too gobsmacked by my present or what?'

'All you want when you come round here,' goes Shithead, 'is drink and nosh.'

'All I want is you to shut it.'

'Fuck off pus-head,' goes Sharon.

Mum made a pot of rosie then we all sat down and started clocking a video.

Then the door started coming off its hinges.

Before they even got their axe through it I was up the back bedroom and out the window.

From our floor you always could drop down the ground. Taking care there was no broken glass under. Sometimes you rolled over a few times breaking the fall. This time I dropped on my plates then went on my knees and that was it.

Looking at it this way. Number one, nobody ever put an axe through our door before. Number two, it was never the style of any villains I heard of excepting maybe Old Bill. Number three, for definite if it was Old Bill I never wanted to know.

Number four, there was no one out the back so it was never Old Bill, always covered the back. Number five, only bastards I knew crazy enough for this one were bandits out of Pakistan and one of them was visiting our manor right now.

Clocking it like that it made sense for a hasty exit.

Course they might do a bit of shooting and looting. Lot of difference it made me being there, I was never a one-man army. It made a lot more mileage fucking off out and saving it for another day. Always a chance when they never made me there they reckoned they got the wrong flat and apologised and went next door.

I belled Old Bill on the mobile then skulked around the back till they rolled up. By then there were several motors going off the front with a bit of banging and a bit of screeching. I went up the boozer a couple of hours for letting events calm down.

'JESUS NICKY!'

'NICKY THE FUCK YOU PLAYING AT!'

'Nicky them was real mean geezers, you hear what I'm saying?' That was our Sharon.

'JESUS NICKY!' Mum never liked you forgetting what she turned round and said so she was after repeating it.

'NICKY YOU BASTARD YOU THREATEN MY CHILD'S LIFE OR WHAT YOU BASTARD!' Kelly forgetting I got a half share in the nipper too.

'Dad it was bleedin' brilliant they got rifles!'

Sharon's kid never did turn round and say a lot. Now they got him out in the kitchen doing the washing up.

There was one geezer missing.

'And where's Shithead?' I goes.

'They bleeding took bleeding Henry bleeding hostage!' goes Mum.

'They kidnapped Shithead?' I goes incredulous.

144

'They bleeding kidnapped him!'

'The fuck happened?'

'You bleeding saw what happened Nicky. They broke in here with that axe, now we got to get the Council put a new door in. They bleeding screamed and yelled at us like there's no tomorrow. Six of them! One of them shouted they wanted you!'

'They think Shithead was me or what?'

'Course they did! They never clocked any bleeding geezer only Henry so they lifted him! Straight off!'

I started cackling. Sharon in the bargain. It never seemed very likely, still Mum believed it. Now she was leaking and shaking like she was gutted.

'Tell them we never want him back,' goes Sharon.

'Tell them we pay the ransom for them to keep him,' I turned round and said.

Mum blubbing some more.

'Nicky you're such a fucking bastard,' went Kelly. 'You can't see your mum's upset or what?'

I was upset in the bargain. Fact was I was bleeding terrified. Geezers were out for me, hostage or what they were out for me.

Still there was no cause to stop having a good laugh. They got Shithead. Either they reckoned he was me, seeing as all white geezers looked the same. Or they just took him for another kidnap when he was handy. Or they were just vex. Either way they took Shithead and that was never bad.

'Mum you make another pot of tea or what?' I goes.

CHAPTER TWENTY-TWO

I TOOK A cab up Stoke Newington, far off as you could get.
Time used to be I lifted a motor for distances. Now I was
too old and anyhow Noreen was likely for mashing up my
short and curlies. Bus up Stoke Newington took longer than
a slow week on remand. I got a minicab off the market and
fucked off out.

Stoke Newington was where you went when you made it
out of Walthamstow and you were a teacher or a brief or you
worked on websites. Footballer or builder or gangster you
went the opposite direction up Chigwell. Stoke Newington
got Asian vegetarian restaurants on every doorstep. Saved
them going down Green St where the Asians lived.

Stoke Newington got England's bentest nick. Old Bill there
made a corkscrew look like a ruler. They reckoned they cleaned
it up now. They never got the Jif on it too serious then. You
were black and breathing, step out the door and it was likely
for possession with intent and say hello to the inside of a cell.

Marigold lived up Stoke Newington off Church St.

She was our teacher when we were hardly up to robbing
age. Marigold was wild. Outside Walthamstow she was the
only straight person I got the acquaintance of.

I paid off the cabbie on Stoke Newington High St and wandered round till I made sure I was clean. You wanted to keep your straight mates you took care you never took any business up their way. Best you never got them totalled, spoil your sanctuary.

Round about six o'clock I hoped Marigold got home from school. She worked up Newham these days. Walthamstow got too soft she reckoned, not deprived enough. Glutton for hardship was Marigold. Ought to be home by six though when the dark lights came down over Newham.

I banged on her door with little sharp taps like you did polite with your teacher. She got a flat upstairs.

One time I came round Marigold's a few years back when I was in serious water. No place to go except your old teacher. We ended up sharing a shag. My knees still shook when I thought on it. It was sex like they just invented it that morning. Tell the truth I never quite recovered.

She came on down the stairs and the door opened and she stood there. Brilliant.

Pause.

'Nicky Burkett,' she turned round and said.

'Marigold.'

'Don't tell me. This is a social call. Or you're in deep shit.'

'Not exactly deep shit Marigold, more like a spot of aggravation and I got to make a bit of an exit.'

When she taught Vinnie and Jimmy and Dean and me she got big hair about four foot long. When I got my event with her it was down to four millimetres. Now it was like six inches, oily and spiky.

When we were kids you never got a teacher with a ring in her hooter. Not even Marigold.

'You got a ring in your hooter now Marigold,' I added.

'I can see I taught you observation, Nicky. You'd better come in then, hadn't you?'

147

'Appreciate it Marigold.'

We went upstairs to her gaff. When she lived on Coppermill Lane she got bare boards and hippie carpets on the walls and a French boyfriend on account of she taught French. Now she still got bare boards on the floor only she got bare white walls and wooden furniture and she was playing Tibetan monks singing or so she reckoned. Out in the kitchen she got a pot of barley cooking. She slept on the bare boards. She was one of a kind was Marigold.

'Tea, Nicky? Or will you just doss down right away, get some sleep and then out again?'

I sensed a spot of friction here.

'Marigold I ain't got no one else to ask. And seeing as you were my French teacher and such a brilliant bird and that, and me innocent on this one only needing to get out of the borough right sharp on account of there's geezers on my case, I only kind of wondered I could kip here a couple of days till the old hoo-ha dies down, you hear what I'm saying?'

'I hear you Nicky.'

Then she cackled.

'Oh, all right then. But you know the conditions. Two or three days no more, and you bring no trouble this way, right?'

'Course not Marigold you know me. And you're a diamond, I ain't lying to you, bleeding diamond.'

'Thank you Nicky. Tea then?'

'Don't mind if I do.'

TT was the mastermind. DSTT Holdsworth out of Chingford.

TT went on management courses and business courses and computer courses. Still he was only a bleeding sergeant. They got bigger ranks in for the business. They made TT the liaison person.

The nobs sat behind him while TT gave his spiel.

They wanted us to go round Walthamstow nick by Greenleaf Rd. Walthamstow was kind of a sub-nick, like all the serious grief went down in Chingford or Leyton. They reckoned they wanted us all up Walthamstow nick where they got a quiet room for a talk. I reckoned not. I had too many talks in quiet rooms. We met by Mr and Mrs Malik.

There was TT and the nobs and we were waiting on representatives of Kamran's employers. There was Mr and Mrs Malik and Alia. There was me. Then there was our Sharon, family occasion. Mum we kept locked up back home. Last and most there was Rameez.

Rameez was never flavour of the month round the Asian community up Queen's Rd. Down the mosque every day, send your daughters up Walthamstow Girls School and you reckon you done enough to keep the hooligans out of their knickers.

I belled Rameez on his mobile and caught him by the boozer on Markhouse Rd sorting out a few Pernods. We never made our meet up the Ambala yet. Then I belled Alia and she agreed I took him by her mum's.

Mr and Mrs were so upset on account of their Kamran they forgot to give me a second cup of tea. I never met Asians forgot the second cup. Most times they stood over you and very near shoved it down with a funnel. So they were upset and then they got Rameez on their doorstep like the plague visiting. Still they got the tea out for him. One cup.

They yacked away in Urdu and I looked intelligent. Every now and then one of them went 'one crore pounds sterling' or 'kidnap' or 'shoot the bastards innit?' Rameez went the last one not Mrs Malik.

The door bell went again. Alia went out the room and came back with two suits.

It was Kamran's bosses. White geezers with expensive tailors. Rameez's hooter started quivering and his hand went to his mugger's pocket.

'Please come in Mr Dickens and Mr Palumbo,' goes Mrs Malik. 'Would you like tea?'

'No thank you Mrs Malik, we just had one a couple of hours ago,' Dickens turned round and said.

'A couple of hours?' she goes kind of hysterical. 'A couple of hours ago? You must be dying of thirst!'

'Drink the bleeding tea,' I went. Rule number one: drink it.

'Er, yes, of course, yes, beg your pardon.' Kind of an arsy city type, not your Essex boy more you came out of Surrey up Waterloo.

'We went up to Chingford police station first,' he went like it was Lapland.

'They knock you around in them cells?' I asked.

'Shut it Nicky,' goes TT.

'They think there is a conspiracy to kidnap people of Pakistani origin who work for city firms.'

'This is exactly why we are all here now,' goes TT making his play, the nobs getting restive. 'Thank you all for coming.'

While Dickens was yacking Palumbo was making a dent in the gathia they brought with the tea. It was chili gathia so he started coughing and choking and his mince pies leaking and he was drooling into his tea.

'Detective Sergeant Holdsworth,' went one of the nobs, 'will summarise the situation.' He was big from the Yard. Wore a hat. Last time I clocked him was when they were after lifting the bent Chief Super out of Chingford. These were serious hitters.

'There are two kidnappees,' goes TT.

'Correct,' I goes.

'This is an unusual situation. In this country kidnapping is a non-frequent commercialist hazard.' He was getting his press statement a rehearsal.

'Give us a fuckin' break TT,' I turned round and said. 'Mr and Mrs don't need no fuckin' sermon you hear what I'm saying?'

'Who is this youth?' went Dickens. I was pleased with the youth.

'He is very good friend,' goes Mrs. 'He saved our son and your employee when he was in Pakistan. Now he has lost a dear relative also in this latest kidnapping.'

'Oh I see.'

'Listen to what the man says,' went the big man.

'One of the kidnappings was fortuitous,' TT turned round and said.

'Top word TT,' I goes. 'Fuck does it mean?'

'We have reason to believe that the person they were targeting was not the person they seized. But they do not know this.'

Everyone just as confused as each other now.

'We do not know how much they will demand as a ransom for this other person, or even if they will demand a ransom at all. To be honest, and there is nothing else we can be in this situation, they may just decide to kill him.'

'Yes!' hissed Sharon.

'Meanwhile – and this is not because we are in any way out of our depth – we have decided to utilise every spade in our resources. We are therefore in immediate contact with a gentleman from Pakistan who deals with kidnappings every day of the week and who may be able to share his expertise with us in order to facilitate the common delivery of our objectives.'

151

Palumbo was weeping now, on account of the gathia not TT.

'He should be arriving postwith. His name is Imran Khan.'

'The cricketer,' went Dickens.

'Not the same Imran Khan,' goes Mr Malik.

'No?'

'He is not the same one believe you me. Imran Khan is too busy with his hospital and his white wife.'

I gave TT the number for old Imran in the bargain. Reckoned they never got the face for talking down Jamil Khan Jamal. Credit to TT and his guvnors, they sent for Imran straight off out of taxpayer's dosh.

'And this man Jamil Khan,' went Dickens, 'is he related to either of the Imran Khans?'

They all got the giggles then, brought a spot of light relief.

'Listen geezer,' I goes.

'Excuse me?'

'We got to have like a two-bit plan here.'

'I'm not sure I agree.' Dickens never rated me high on his favometer. Asians he could handle like Martians. White trash though was more uncomfortable.

'First we negotiate. Trust me. I seen it happen. Then we whack 'em. Only the clever money says we get the second bit in first.'

'Hrmph,' goes one of the Old Bill. Time to fade my gob.

'There is something on the negotiations we need to discuss urgently with you,' goes TT to Kamran's guvnors. 'Perhaps in private.'

'In private?' goes Sharon, clocked I needed an assist here. 'In private so Mr and Mrs Malik never get it? And what about me and my bro here, lost a dear departed member of our family?'

'You want to know if they pay the dosh?' goes Rameez.

'Well …' goes TT.

152

'What?' Dickens turned round and said. Palumbo still snivelling.

'They want to know you reckon Mrs Malik's boy worth a hundred large,' I went. 'You like to pay the fee some of us never got to be involved further, you get me?' About Kamran that was. Shithead they could keep.

'Oh …' went Dickens.

'Yeah,' I goes.

'I don't know …'

'Yeah.'

'We shall have to discuss …'

'Yeah.'

'The circumstances are complicated.'

'Yeah?'

'Naturally we place a very high priority on the health and safety of our staff. We are second to none in this respect.'

'Yeah.'

'At the same time we have a responsibility to our share-holders.'

'And Kamran not being very important …'

'We are accountable to them and they will want to see us strike a balance.'

'Next time they better kidnap some director geezer, am I right?'

Then Mr Malik stepped in. He never gave up on the politeness only he was knowing how the shelves were stacked for some Asian kid in the city.

'Inspector,' he turned round and said to the Yard. 'We must start to negotiate with the kidnappers. For my son's welfare we must start to talk although the money will not be forthcoming. My family does not have this money. Perhaps we can talk about a smaller amount or some other solution.'

Old Bill kind of awkward only expecting it. 'We will not give in to terrorists,' he goes straight from the book.

We all waited.

'However, in this case we will, having been given your agreement, begin to negotiate as and when we can. At the moment we do not have a contact route. There will be some hard decisions to make and it will be useful to hear of the experiences of the gentleman from Pakistan when he arrives. If we give them the money they will be back again but of course if the money had been available we would have borne in mind the views of the family and the prospects for the victim's future.'

Mrs started leaking. 'Please get my son back,' she went.

'Rameez,' I goes, 'we best have that meet you were on about, yeah?'

CHAPTER TWENTY-THREE

MUM GOT A letter in the bargain.
'Dear Lady,' it went.

'Ain't you for a start off then Mum,' went Sharon. 'Dear Lady, you pay one lakh pounds sterling for Mr Burkett.'

'One lakh!' I went.

'What that Nicky?' goes Sharon.

'One bleedin' lakh! Kamran he was one bleedin' crore!'

'How much is one bleedin' lakh Nicky?'

I couldn't remember what a fucking lakh was. 'Fuck sight less than one bleedin' crore,' I went.

'Yeah but that's for Shithead Nicky. Look at the state of him.'

'Oh yeah.'

'He ain't a fine specimen of geezer like you and me Nicky, right?'

'You reckon they got me in person they got to ask at least two crore, hear what I'm saying?'

'Count on it. Whatever a fuckin' crore is, they ask two of 'em.'

'They think Henry's you Nicky,' goes Mum stating the bleeding obvious and starting on the blubbing again. 'What they never took a proper butcher's at you up Pakistan or what?'

'Seems like it Mum. Too bleedin' quick for 'em.'

'They bleedin' want their eyes tested is all I can bleedin' say.'

'No problem far as I'm concerned. What else it says in that letter Mum?'

'One lakh pounds sterling carry in a bag from Kwiksave.'

'Easy peasy then, know what I mean? No grief.'

'We ain't got no poxy Kwiksave bag! I went up Sainsbury's this week!'

'Serve you bleedin' right. Only they reckon Kwiksave so better be Kwiksave innit? Pop down there dinner time. Next question?'

'Take the bag to Ilford on Saturday.'

'Nicky, how we gonna take that bag when we don't know how much one lakh is? Leaving aside we ain't got the dosh whatever it is.'

'Don't make no difference how much it is. We fill it up with newspaper.'

'Yeah?'

'Yeah.'

'Then what?'

'We get them sorted.'

'Yeah?'

'Yeah.'

'And what happens to Henry?'

'Take his chances. First off we hold up proceedings. We tell Old Bill. We give them a smack. Then when old Imran comes from Pakistan we tell him in the bargain. Let him do all that negotiating. They rescue Henry. And Kamran.'

'Nicky,' goes Sharon, 'how come you're such a big man all suddenly? You been taking them tablets or what?'

'I got Rameez.'

'Rameez?'

'Rameez.'

'You reckon Rameez is one big enough geezer for these geezers?'

'Maybe. Him and his posse.'

'Hmph. And how you going to get Rameez co-operate? You pay him big spends what you ain't got?'

'I gave that plan consideration. Then I went to Plan B consideration. I tell him you want to marry him.'

'You what?'

'I tells him you want to marry him.'

'Nicky you all right in the bonce? You gone brown bread in the brain area or what? Marry Rameez, you reckon I marry Rameez? Jesus I ain't never met no one got married. Let alone to Rameez. Rameez? He ain't bad for a quick one Nicky but he ain't hardly Brad Pitt.'

'Don't never have to be true Sharon. You just reckon you tell his mum and dad. How your relations are with him. And him on a promise back home like.'

'Ah …'

'You with me?'

'Yeah …'

'Seeing as there's this bird up Lahore.'

'Her he's always going on about while he's poking me.'

'That the one.'

'Second cousin. Good family. Very clean. Like he reckon I ain't none of them things except good enough when he want a fast up-and-under.'

'You get my meaning?'

'So he does the business with his boys or we go round his house …'

'Except Nicky …'

157

She paused while we thought on the glitch situation.

'Yeah,' I goes.

'You with me?'

'Yeah.'

'Problem being, Rameez does the business too good maybe we get fucking Shithead back.'

'Got to be a downside Sharon. Nothing in life ain't perfect, know what I mean? Anyhow keep Mum happy.'

Mum starts leaking loud again. All this time she was sobbing quiet in a corner. Now she heard Shithead's name she started back on the big boo-hoos.

'Who's gonna be the one tell Rameez, Nicky?'

'You sis. Course. You being intimate and that.'

'Get lost Nicky. You such a clever dick on the verbals. Your job mate.'

'Shit.'

Mickey Cousins was coming down the market with his two boys, Tweedledum and fucking Tweedledummer.

I was going up the market with Jimmy Foley. He was after telling me how he was never getting any birds lately. Jimmy reckoned how on two occasions in the past he got birds coming out his arse. Each time it was after he was getting shot. All the bits of stuff in Walthamstow came round then, all wanting to cuddle up and clock his exit wounds. Recent times though he reckoned the borough was a woman desert.

'Nicky it just ain't reasonable,' he went. 'Them birds just ain't coming across, know what I mean? I tried every old tart on the manor near as. Now we got over twenty years old they all turn round and say they got a kid or a bit of work or they hanging round some gangster. What happened to all them fluffies Nicky? How come just because they got some kid or a number up west they never want to spread it around no more?'

'You just too old Jimmy. Your age and you want birds, you got to have plenty of lettuce or a bleeding great apparatus mate. You never got them, you too fuckin' old.'

'Jesus Nicky I'm only twenty-four.'

'Lettuce?'

'Potless Nicky you know that.'

'And that apparatus?'

'Well, kind of average.'

'No chance then mate. Waste away for lack of use.'

We carried on up the market.

Then I clocked them.

'Hold on up Jimmy,' I goes. 'You may get your opportunity geezer.'

'My oppo for what Nicky?'

'You reckon you got to get shot for pulling them birds? Anything else do? Break a couple of pins, do any good?'

'Doubt it Nicky. Them holes is what they like where them bullets went. Run their little tongues all round I'm telling you.'

'Pity. On account of we got a situation here.'

We faced them up.

Mickey Cousins was a bent motor dealer out of North Chingford. Least that was his front for the law. Out the back he dealt all the business you got going. We crossed a few times. He never took a shine to me after we broke his legs.

Tweedledum and fucking Tweedledummer were his muscle for daily jobs. They were never there for the thinking. Fact was they made Jimmy Foley look like monster mind.

'Well if it ain't Nicky Burkett,' goes Mickey. 'And his little mate.'

'All right Mickey?' goes Jimmy.

Mickey was limping where we smacked him one time.

'Still hurting Mickey?' I goes. 'Still got them aches and pains? Arthritis set in yet or what?'

'You little fucker I reckon your number came up this time you little bastard. You pissed on my chips once too often my friend. I reckon you down shit creek without a paddle you hear me?'

'Jimmy,' I goes. 'Them two at the sides is yours. I take the cripple in the middle.'

'You got it good and proper this time,' Mickey carries on regardless. 'You met your Wembley now and no mistake.'

'Waterloo Mickey,' I goes.

'Eh?'

'You met your Waterloo,' I turned round and said. 'Not Wembley Mickey.'

'Shut the fuck up. What you never knew when you was fartarsing round Pakistan was, I happen to be in a bit of business with a certain Jamil Khan Jamal.'

Jesus.

'Who?' I goes.

'And you been treading on a few toes all round, am I right?'

'Who me? I ain't got a fuckin' starter what the fuck you're on about.'

'And you went up Pakistan like a little snow white innocent, yes?'

'Thought about getting married is all Mickey. Reckon I pick up a wife somewhere, good clean bird up Pakistan, nice family, know what I mean?'

'You reckon I came down off the fuckin' winkle barge or what you little fucker? I knows all about your game Nicky Burkett. And I knows how it ain't never you that Jamil Khan Jamal got kidnapped, on account of I sees you here in front of me. So I reckon when they got their cashback for whoever the fuck they did get up there, they come after looking for you

160

you little fucker. I gives them the word and Christmas only come early.'

'You in the fuckin' kidnap game now Mickey? The fuck it got to do with your bit of work?'

'Like I said, we got certain interests in common like a few commodities. None of your fucking business anyhow. Now maybe we won't be teaching you a lesson today, bit crowded. Get the fuck out of my road and we come for you a bit later.'

'Jimmy,' I goes.

'Yeah Nicky?'

'Teach them a bit of respect, you got me?'

Jimmy clocked what I clocked. Behind them Rameez was giving it prowl. Not a lot went down on the market without Rameez heard it kind of quick. Most the stalls paid him protection and they all got mobiles and he got his gaff nearby. And he got Afzal and Aftab and Javed standing right there like they were fasting.

It was all over very sharp before Old Bill came out their office fifty yards off.

Aftab slapped Tweedledum with a rice flail on the collar bone. Afzal gave Tweedledummer a jab up the kidneys put him in the hospital a week. Rameez knew where Mickey hurt most on account of he did him the first injury. He tapped him around the knees and back a few times left Mickey roaring.

Then they were gone, melted.

Jimmy and I carried on up the market looking for a bit of stuff for him.

I knew it was never long before Jamil heard the news so we got to be moving.

CHAPTER TWENTY-FOUR

I TOOK MY capo up the Ambala for the meet.
Fact was I took a few extra capos for being on the safe side.

There was Jimmy Foley. There was Elvis Littlejohn smooth as a cucumber. There was Wayne Sapsford rolled up in the Audi he lifted out of Woodford, and Dean Longmore always handy he wanted to retail the Audi after. There was Shelley Rosario for scandalising the management, bit of a good girl. Then I brought Paulette James, six foot and running for England, on account of she was the only two-footed creature Rameez was leery of.

He was scared of leeches though so I heard.

We took up post first in the Ambala. Rameez came down with Aftab and Afzal and Javed. We were seated got our nosh already off the counter.

'Jesus Nicky you bring all your friends and relations, kind of an ambush or what? You not feel safe in Pakistani house?'

'You reckoned bring my capo Rameez. Never decided which one was my capo so I brought the bunch. Anyhow you went how that capo was there for the thinking. My number one Jimmy ain't so strong on the thinking so I brought a thinking back-up. All together ought to have some thoughts innit?'

They got their grub and brought it over and parked.

'All right Aftab?'

'All right Jimmy?'

'All right Afzal?'

'All right Wayne?'

'All right Javed?'

'All right Dean?'

'All right Aftab?'

'All right Elvis?'

'All right Afzal?'

'All right Paulette?'

'Enough boys!' went Rameez. Shelley he never rated. Paulette he pretended was never there on account of the shivers. So there was only boys.

Food up the Ambala was decent. Better down Green St. Still for Leyton High Rd you got to say it passed the test.

I got my retaliation in.

'Rameez my friend,' I went like the duce. 'Almost my brother, know what I mean?'

'Yeah ... ?'

'You and me being as we're nearly blood relations we never be separated, am I right?'

'Eh?'

'Of course I knows you is a businessman through and through no mistaking. On the other hand, you is loyal first. I says to my capo Jimmy, Rameez is loyal.'

'Loyal,' goes Jimmy.

'You in a fix, Rameez be there. You want your brother beside you, he there with his slicer. No doubting old Rameez.'

Rameez's posse a spot puzzled on that one on account of one time he chased me round the borough two years after I lifted his brand new motor by accident.

'Like I say you being about to be family and that ...'

163

'Hold on up Nicky,' Rameez goes.

'Yes my brother?'

'The fuck all this about family? You been watching them old mob movies? You ain't even in my band. I a businessman Nicky. You here to put the proposition to me.'

I gobbed on my mushroom bhaji, wiped it round with a bit of nan. Not too dusty. I waited. Trying not to show my legs shaking.

'So you ain't told your boys Rameez.'

'Told them what?'

'About your wedding.'

'Wedding? The fuck wedding? Ain't for years yet, she waiting up Lahore.'

'About my sis? About you and her? For your honour?'

'Honour? The fuck you on about Nicky?'

'My sis reckon you going to marry her now you experienced carnal relations with her. She reckon on account of you so strong on that honour. Got to splice her. Never deflower her without doing the decent or you spoil her rep for her lifetimes.'

'Nicky your Sharon! Deflowered! Jesus Nicky she got a kid six years ago! The fuck you on about deflowered?'

'Sharon reckon you got to tell your mum and dad Rameez. Or else she so in love with you she never be able to hold back any longer and got to have the joy of telling them herself, know what I mean?'

'Nicky you got a whosit in your head? My family clock your Sharon at their door they likely call the RSPCA. Sure as hell they don't got no need for her travelling massage business anyhow.'

Some geezers might take offence Rameez dissing their sister that way, want to teach him his manners. Some geezers might like to get themselves scalped. I preferred finishing up my meal.

Rameez's dad drove a No. 97 bus. Rameez's mum ran the lunch club up the Asian Centre. Rameez's sisters were fucking beautiful only they made you goodnight about seven o'clock and off to their college books. Fuck knows where they got Rameez.

'How you wants it Rameez,' I turned round and said. 'No problem geezer. Only I'm telling you Sharon she reckon she just got to go by your mum and dad and tell them she about to be their daughter on account of you put it in her so good you got lovesick something painful Rameez. She talking wedding bells so quick there ain't even no baby showing …'

'Baby! She got some baby!'

'I ain't saying she got some baby Rameez. I ain't never saying that. Not for definite mind. Only kind of joyous innit your mum and dad got a twinkle in their eye?'

'The fuck Nicky, she ain't even a Muslim!'

'She reckon she take lessons.'

'Fuck's sake.'

I got to tread careful. Give him the full shame in front his crew and he got to stick me. He got plenty of honour, you only got to point it where it mattered.

'Course …'

'Course what?'

'Course I could put in a word.'

He gave the stabbing stare.

Then he picked his blade out his pocket.

'You don't happen to be meaning I line up your side save your skin off them kidnap merchants?'

'Well …'

'You get a result there and it don't happen ever being mentioned again like?'

'Maybe Rameez. Just maybe.'

He stood up. His mates all stood up.

Then he sat down again. His mates all sat down again.

'Fuck you Nicky,' he went.

Meant I won.

'You well out of order, digging me out like I'm on my jacks here.'

'Never Rameez. Not you mate. Not digging you out.'

'I could waste you faster than a moody fiver.'

'Course Rameez. No problem feller, know what I mean?'

'I could knock you. Promise I be there then give a no-show. You be there on your tod.'

'You never do that.'

'Fuck you Nicky.'

'Thank you Rameez.'

'I do it. For your honour.'

'For your honour my brother.'

'For comradeship. For Walthamstow.' He got to find a good reason.

'Hear what you're saying.'

He picked at his rice. They all picked at their rice. Then he lifted his bonce.

'What time and place you plan to meet them fuckers?' he goes. 'They got a ransom note for Kamran or what?'

'I never heard yet. Only for Shithead. And they only turned round and went take the dosh to Ilford on Saturday in a Kwiksave bag. Reckon they be following, give you the instructions when you get there. Want you on their patch for the business.'

'We keep in touch with them over Kamran. Could be same time same place, might be different.'

'No problem.'

'And that Imran Khan be here. They clock him and they going to be plenty vex I'm telling you.'

166

'True words brother.'

'Shit.'

'Look at it this way. You sort this situation Rameez and your rep going to be massive round here, know what I mean?'

'Don't you be sweetening no fucking pill Nicky. You put one over on me here mister. I not going to forget that.' Then he grinned.

Rameez was never big on stressing his sense of humour. When he grinned he got meaningful molars.

I was leaving little pools of sweat round my feet. When I stood up to go I nearly fell in them.

* * *

Later on Marigold cooked me a meal out of barley.

Marigold was thin as a pin and fit as a flasher. She went swimming before breakfast by her school. Only needed a few drugs and she'd be perfect.

'What's it all about, Nicky?' she goes. We were sat at the table in the evening.

I gave her the brief on my activities. I gave her most of it straight up.

'My my,' she goes. 'So you really did stop stealing cars and all that? You're just a vigilante now part-time, is that it?'

'Marigold,' I goes pained, 'do me a favour innit? Twenty-four now and that. Can't be lifting motors. You got your respect.'

'And you just shoot people instead now, is that it?'

Woman was on my case.

'I ain't never shot one single geezer,' I turned round and said.

'No?'

'Well …' I remembered one I shot in the foot, escaped my mind one moment. 'Not so he flaked anyhow. You knows me

Marigold, I aren't no shooter and Noreen she's a straight goer she won't be doing with none of that. And all that French you were after teaching us, you can't be learning all that and then thieving, am I right?'

'It didn't seem to stop you for several years. Maybe it had a delayed effect. Anyway I'm very glad you're a good citizen now. That means you're handing everything over to the police then, are you? No vigilante jobs, no gang warfare, no taking the law into your own hands?'

'Not my hands Marigold. Rameez's hands is the plan. Can't never be leaving it to the law you know that. Kamran be in bits and pieces before the law arrive.'

'Is it better if Rameez does it? Is there a difference?'

'Course there is girl! Things go wrong, Rameez gets shafted not me innit? Not very likely mind, being a bit fast himself with the shafting is Rameez.'

'So you won't be going along at all?'

'Well in an observer role Marigold. Like them UN geezers, right? See fair play and that, direct the traffic.'

'I'm sure you will.'

'No problem you be sure of that. No problem at all.'

'And you won't come back here arrested? Or mutilated?'

'Nah. Like to keep all my bits attached, know what I mean?'

I went off to my mattress. Never got round to buying beds did Marigold. You stayed round her gaff you got to like kipping on a bleeding mattress. Wanted a pillow you got to make it yourself. Then you got to be sleeping very sound in the morning, case she snatched you out for some running or a spot of underwater weight training or vegan aerobics or whatever the fuck else. I got ten hours kip ready for some more of that crusading.

CHAPTER TWENTY-FIVE

B E SEEN IN Walthamstow I needed a spot of security. Rameez was one thing. On my side for now, better than being my oppo. Only when Rameez heard about a deal going down or a geezer needed slicing or some bird wanting it put up her, Rameez got a higher calling. I needed someone to watch over me a couple of days.

I got off the bus and went in the Victoria for a pint of Murphy's. The Victoria was next to the Granada, what they changed to the EMD these days. It was kind of hidden. I reckoned even they found the entrance Jamil's boys could get kind of intimidated by the vibes up the Victoria.

Last time some stranger went in the Victoria the Coronation was on the TV. Now they got the Gaelic football on. They got serious people up the Victoria doing some serious drinking while they watched. They never wanted the football or the drinking disturbed by some stranger wandering in and talking.

I got my pint and huddled in a corner feeling a little bit of security. Then a big bit of security strolled in the door. My answer just found me and no messing.

Terry the tattoo artist was as wide as he was long and as deep as he was wide. It took about twenty minutes to walk round him. You dropped him from an aeroplane and he bounced. He did martial arts I never heard of. He trained every day. He entered combat in Germany. He gave lectures in California. He hurt geezers in many countries.

He was tattooed all over.

Well, all you could clock. He got tattoos over his arms and his shoulders. He got tattoos on his bonce. He got tattoos that snarled and sneered at you.

Terry wore a gold chain round his neck. About ten foot long, it went round once. Weighed as much as a motor. I could never lift it. Most geezers up Walthamstow, you wore your gold open down the market and you got relieved of the weight. It was up Amsterdam before you could say fuck me. Terry he never had to worry.

He bought a short one at the bar then he clocked me. Came over my corner. Terry was allowed to talk in the Victoria.

'Nicky Burkett,' he goes.

'All right Terry?'

'Mind if I sit down?'

No one ever minded.

'Words reaches me,' he started off, 'that you have been involved in some disturbances Nicky Burkett.'

'Now you mention it,' I goes. 'Reckon I have.'

'Spot of bother?'

'Spot of bother.'

'And words also reaches me,' he carries on, 'that Walthamstow is playing a home match against Pakistan.'

'Yeah ...' I goes.

I was beginning to see light.

'Them fuckers,' he turned round and said. 'Them fuckers from Asia is wanting to devastate our Asian people.'

'Right Terry.'

170

'Our Walthamstow Asian people.'

Terry was very patriotic. He loved Walthamstow. He loved Walthamstow people. Even when he got to get severe with them and give them a good pasting he loved them.

'From Walthamstow,' he went again. He was so indignant his tattoos were bursting out his shoes, all the snakes and dragons and women curving and waving and biting.

'True words Terry mate,' I turned round and said. 'Them messing serious with our Walthamstow Asian boys. Born and bred Terry. Went to school up McEntee. Went to court up the Town Hall. Shop down the market.'

Terry was born and bred in the bargain. Difference was he was so bad not even McEntee entertain his education. He got most his reading off the warrants from the court. He swore they sent him birthday cards him being their leading customer.

'Them fuckers,' he goes.

I let him think on how they were dissing our manor. He sipped his short one.

'And now they after mashing you up in the bargain Nicky, am I right?'

'Been a bit of a problem Terry,' I admitted. 'Not so important beside what they doing to Walthamstow, course. Kind of midgy beside that.'

'You all alone wandering about?' he asked.

'Yeah.'

'Not got your lemon curd with you I hope?'

'Try to keep Noreen out of it Terry.'

'Maybe you best stay round me a couple hours, you get my meaning?'

'Appreciate it Terry. Do me a favour.'

Kind of a big favour. I was coming over kind of shitless. Could have started blubbing right there.

'I owes you Terry,' I turned round and said.

171

'You don't owe me nothing Nicky, I ain't doing this for you mate. Doing this for Walthamstow.'

'Fair play Terry. No problem mate.' I didn't give a fuck why he was doing it.

'You come round my studio, right?'

We walked out of there ten feet tall. Both of us got a crick looking up at six foot geezers only we went out of there looking down on the 97 bus. Least I did. Terry went out casual. They might take him with an intercontinental missile only no one was ever going to shaft him on a mugging.

Terry used to do his business by the market before he moved up. Now his shop was a couple of minutes away up Hoe St and round the corner. We shanked up there. He took up the pavement and I slunk.

We made polite conversation about the good old days of football hooliganism and detention centres.

Then he went sudden still.

'Jesus,' he turned round and said.

'Problem Terry?'

'Fucking problem? You fucking see what I'm seeing Nicky?'

'Dunno Terry. 275 bus. Couple of birds. Roland The Ferret. Nothing else mate.'

'Roland The Fucking Ferret …'

'Yeah?'

'Roland The Fucking Ferret Gambon dealing on my corner, am I right?'

Roland The Ferret Gambon was a dealer in a BMW. Full-time crack and a spot of brown. He was very mean news. He was not a friendly geezer.

Terry went kind of vacant. He went in another dimension. One moment I reckoned there was a Jackie Chan kind of wail on the path. He moved up to that BMW (illegal parked, single

172

yellow line) and he put his mitt in the window where Roland had it wound down for doing a deal with some sixteen-year-old crackhead.

Now that door was locked. Only that was never a problem for Terry. He took that door off the motor. Snarled and it was gone. In the gutter.

Then he pulled Roland out the motor in the bargain. He pulled him up very close. So close their hooters were touching. Some geezers when they wanted to give you a warning they got you up so close you got cross-eyed. That was never close enough for Terry. His hooter and Roland's hooter were like Siamese twins.

Roland was known to shaft a geezer for sneezing somewhere near his powder.

'You fucking dealing on my corner Roland Fucking Ferret Fucking Gambon?'

'Your corner Terry?'

'My corner Roland.'

'Jeez Terry.'

'Fucking deal on that corner over fucking there. Or fucking deal on some fucking corner in Australia. Only you don't fucking never deal on my fucking corner here, am I right?'

'Jeez Tel, sorry mate. My driver here he ain't got no fucking sense of direction.'

Terry eyeballed him. Couldn't rub their eyeballs together while their hooters were touching only he got close as possible. Roland was never in any doubt about his feelings.

Terry held him there thirty seconds. Then he put him back in the motor.

They drove off without their door.

'I tell you what Nicky,' Terry turned round and said. 'I got to police my fucking corner. Only way mate. I run a clean ship here, know what I mean?'

'Got you Terry.'

'Clean fucking ship. No problem.'

We thought about that.

'Now we go in and get a cup of tea, yeah?'

'Right Terry.' We went indoors and up his stairs.

Up his shop he got all the state of the art tattooing gear. Then round the walls he got photos. Of tattoos. Most of them on birds. Arms legs shoulders feet and a part of their anatomy I never clocked enough of. They got tattoos all round there. It was obvious I missed out on learning a lot about birds.

On one wall he got a prison VO. On visits you were allowed three adults and they got to be named on the VO. This VO on the wall Terry got framed. He was one of the names. Other two were Tony Mortimer and Brian Harvey out of E17 when they were mega. Terry took them up the nick one day for a chat with Reggie Kray.

He made the rosie and while we drank it his punters started coming in. Taking a butcher's, getting up the bottle. Black geezer came in. Terry rubbed his arm, explained a problem with a skin condition how some black people need to be careful with tattoos. Made an appointment. Couple of birds came in wanted their ankles done right off. Terry made an appointment.

'Always make an appointment,' he went to me.

'Always?'

'Always.'

'Everyone?'

'Everyone. Lennox Lewis comes in, got to make an appointment. Sharon Stone, got to make an appointment. Fucking Queen wanders in, don't matter if I'm free all day, she wants a fucking corgi on her bum or whatsit, she still got to make an appointment.'

'You reckon she wants a corgi on her bum Terry?'

'Stands to reason, am I right? Queen comes swanning up Hoe St, only one reason, wants a corgi on her bum. Still she got to come back next day.'

'And the Duke? Or Charlie?'

'Charlie probably want some woman on his belly only he still don't get it right off. See, they got to show respect Nicky. In life we all got to show respect. All of us. You give people what they want straight off, they don't respect you. Am I right?'

'You right Terry.'

We sat there all afternoon. He never did tattoos that day. Just made appointments. Few geezers wandered in for a gab. He gabbed. They showed respect. We drank tea.

'You like this job Terry innit?' I asked eventual.

He paused. 'Let me tell you something Nicky,' he turned round and said. 'This is the greatest game in the world mate. I fucking love it.'

'Yeah?'

'You get paid for being an artist, yeah?'

'Yeah.'

'And you get paid for inflicting pain. There anything better?'

'No Terry. Can't be.'

It was getting late. Nearly time to go home. We were sipping some more rosie when he clocked his CCTV on what was outside his window. Sudden he was off like a fart.

He was down the stairs and out the door. I followed.

Geezer was pissing against the wall.

Two seconds later geezer was flat against the wall. Terry on his case.

'YOU WHAT!' Terry went.

'Wha … ?'

'Where you fuckin' live John?'

175

'Er …'

'Where?!'

'Seventeen Palmerston Rd!'

'Right. Tonight I'm coming round and piss on your fuckin' wall!'

'Sorry Terry. Caught short. Not thinking. Out of the boozer. Course mate. Come round and piss on my house any time Tel.'

And he did.

I stayed safe up Terry's shop two days.

CHAPTER TWENTY-SIX

W E PUT MUM in the frame carrying that Kwiksave bag.
She was the decoy.

They were never likely for taking her out from rifle distance.
Pot Mum and they never got the bag. Close in work we gave
her protection. We put a ring of Rameez's bodies round her.

I belled Alia at her mum and dad's the night before.

'Nicky!' she goes.

'Yeah Alia!' I goes.

'We have got a letter from kidnappers!'

'Very good!'

'Imran Khan is here!'

'Bleeding ace!'

'He says leave it all to him and the police!'

'And what does that letter turn round and say?'

'It says tell the police and we kill Kamran!'

I left her thinking on that one a few moments. Then I went
'And what else it says, Alia?'

'It says they have Kamran and we must wait for further
instructions.'

So they were after clocking how it went down on Shithead
first. Take a butcher's if we got Old Bill involved and check we

put the dosh up front. Drop the small fry in the fat. How we reckoned it anyhow.

'Oh and Nicky …'

'Yes Alia my darlin'?'

'In their letter they put all Kamran's fingernails.'

Eeugh.

I glugged one moment.

'Never you fuss Alia,' I goes. 'He grow some more back no problem. Better than them whole fingers eh, try hard as you like and eat your greens and you still never grow them fingers back on, you hear what I'm saying?'

'I suppose so Nicky.'

'And they maybe never be Kamran's nails anyhow, am I right? Find 'em down the back of the chair or on the street, know what I mean?'

'I suppose so Nicky. Still it is so awful …'

'Make you right girl. Awful innit. You bearing up then or what?'

Always keep sympathetic with the birds. Made them soft for you.

'Yes I am bearing up Nicky. We are all managing. Thank you.'

'No problem girl. Talk to you later.'

'Thank you Nicky.'

So we started on Shithead first, but one thing we reckoned. We knocked them on Shithead and they were likely for whacking Kamran once and for all. We got to deal with Kamran's situation the same time.

Rameez's boys gave Mum the walking escort from Priory Court up to Forest Rd. Bit like the queen. On Forest Rd she got the 123. She sat downstairs, two bodies in front two behind and two beside. They got to clear a few other passengers out the way. When that bus pulled away we came off South Countess

Rd, Rameez and me and Dean Longmore in a Renault Dean borrowed off Wayne Sapsford. Wayne lifted the motor only no point him being chauffeur or you got stopped on the first traffic lights. Dean was half way legit these days so the new Old Bill on the street hardly knew him.

We followed that bus, stopped where it stopped only looking kind of stupid on the North Circular. We got up Ilford. They put a circle round Mum while we went off on a recce.

Plan was they spotted Mum only they clocked from her escort how they were never able to be taking liberties.

While they were working out the next bit for making the drop we were working out what they were working out. Meantime we were working out our next bit first.

Rameez reckoned he got a cunning plan.

Most of Ilford was Asian. North Ilford was where they lived when they made it. Semi-detached like a grave. Ilford Lane was where they lived before they made it and where they did their shopping.

Streets of houses in all directions off the Lane. On the Lane massive groceries selling rice and lentils and beans and ghee and a hundred veg. Sweet shops retailing the best kachories in London. It happened in Ilford Lane. They knew everything you wanted to know and a lot more. I could as near find out their business as get it on with Delia Smith. Rameez though he got his cunning plan.

He left Javed round Mum with his boys. Javed was a very mean fucker and he liked a bit of stabbing. Anyone wiped out Mum, least they knew they were in a scrap.

Advance party before we reached by Ilford Rameez sent Aftab and Afzal and a couple. They were waiting for us.

What he counted on was how Asians never called in Old Bill on a domestic. He reckoned they sorted their business under the hat. No need for publicity.

All Rameez wanted first off was asking a few questions where Jamil Khan Jamal hung his boots and where he got our geezers.

Way it went down it was sweet.

Mum we left up the precinct. Rameez put his other boys in two parties.

Him and two specials Imtiaz and Gulzar went walking in one of their supermarkets on the Lane with the veg. Aftab and Afzal and a couple went in another the same time. No point giving out warnings.

Rameez pulled out his sword.

'Jesus Christ Rameez,' I went.

'He ain't gonna help you on Ilford Lane,' went Rameez. 'All Muslim here.'

His boy Imtiaz got a shooter.

'That an imitation?' I went.

'Imitations no fucking good,' went Imtiaz. 'Don't shoot.'

Fuck.

They never fussed with the till lady on the way in. They left Gulzar guarding her. They went straight up the back in the office. I hung around not too fucking close. Wandered the aisles looking like a customer. Bought me a bit of garlic keep the devil away. In the office there was a geezer and a woman.

There was a crash in that office.

Voices were raised.

I got my garlic now and I was studying the labels on the baked bean tins.

The glass door went in.

Moment's silence. Then more twittering.

Then Rameez and Imtiaz came out.

'Sweet shop,' goes Rameez.

We left that supermarket. Aftab and Afzal came out the other one the same moment. We went down Ilford Lane like the Magnificent Eight. Me the Puny One lagging behind.

'They were very co-operative,' went Rameez.

'Good to hear Rameez.'

'He never control that supermarket. Not one his outlets. But they reckon he use the sweetshop over there.'

'I ain't sure that other place,' goes Aftab. 'I aren't sure they ain't his boys.'

'You got to get serious?'

'Couple of slaps. They reckon they never heard of Jamil.'

'Telling porkies.'

'What I reckon. We go back teach them their manners when we call?'

'They be on their mobiles by now.'

'Yeah.'

'You go round the back that supermarket right quick. Stop them coming. We take the sweetshop.'

'Yeah.'

They went off and we were in that sweet shop.

That sweet shop they got the politest most respectable shopkeepers in the world. Indian sweets all shapes and colours and samosas and kachories and a load of whatsits. Yes madam, yes sir, a pound of this and half a pound of that and a box all tied up with a ribbon.

Rameez was round the back the counter.

'Where you got Jamil Khan Jamal?' he went poking his sword up some biddie's throat. He never swore at her on account of she was a woman.

She never answered. Trying to only it never came out.

Imtiaz and Gulzar pinned a geezer and another bird back on the wall. Imtiaz fired his shooter in the ceiling.

Other bird pointed out the back.

Gulzar stayed by the door and we went in the back.

Sitting there drinking his tea and still reaching for his rifle was Jamil Khan Jamal.

Least we hoped it was him. None of us knew what he looked like. Imtiaz shot him in the shoulder.

'Where you got them you fucker!'

'Where you got them! Now!'

Rameez made with the sword on the neck.

'NOW!'

Jamil was calm as you're likely when you got shot in the shoulder and a sword up your jugular. He was free to clock the odds here. Heroics was never his best shot now.

'Supermarket,' he goes. 'Up road. Kashmir Supermarket.'

Kashmir supermarket was where Aftab and Afzal went calling.

Imtiaz stayed with him. Gulzar by the door. Both for two minutes only. Rameez and me we were off.

We never even reached by that supermarket when we clocked them. Aftab and Afzal coming up the road with Kamran and Shithead.

I never clocked two frightened geezers in my life than Kamran and Shithead in between Aftab and Afzal. They reckoned they were safer with Jamil's boys.

Then they clocked me.

'Nicky Burkett?' goes Kamran.

'All right Kamran?'

'Nicky Burkett?'

'Kamran we went by all this last time up Pakistan. We get the fuck out of here.'

'Nicky Burkett?'

He got bandages on all his fingers this time.

'Got there while they were making an exit,' goes Aftab. 'Went back in. We went after. Found this two.'

'Smart moves,' went Rameez.

Then Shithead found his vocals.

'You?' he went kind of hoarse.

'Pity I got to pick you up in the bargain,' I turned round and said.

'You fucking little bastard, you heap of piss.'

'Gratitude for you.'

'You wait till I get home.'

Just then Dean pulled up in our motor. Rameez whistled and Imtiaz and Gulzar came running. Big Fiat pulled up too and Aftab and Afzal got in. We climbed in the Renault taking Kamran with us.

Shithead could catch the fucking 123.

Only when we got back in Walthamstow we remembered we left Mum and the other boys still on the decoy.

'Shit!' went Rameez.

'Fuck!' I goes, reckoned straight off what he was on about.

He got on the mobile.

'Get a cab,' he went. 'Take Nicky's mum. Drop her by a safe house.'

I gave him Sharon's new gaff. He passed it by them.

'They be coming for us,' he went. 'We be ready for them Nicky but we need a very big assist.'

'Yeah.'

We took Kamran down Queen's Rd. He was still shaking terrible and he never looked like the geezer we knew passed all his exams and was on the books of the Orient one time.

We stood him by his house and rang the bell and got in the motor. When the door opened and his mum came and she cried out and grabbed him we were away.

* * *

We were sat either side her fire kind of drowsy. I got a can and was reading one of her books, gangsters up Marseilles. Marigold sipping on a glass of vino and reading some book by some old bird. Kind of domestic situation.

'Fancy a quick bunk-up then Marigold?' I goes.

She put her finger in the book to hold her place then looked up kind of absent-minded.

'What?' she goes.

'Touch of howsyourfather?' I went. 'Fancy a bit of loving for old times' sake, know what I mean?'

'What?' she goes again.

'Seeing as we did it one time?'

She kept her finger in the book.

'Nicky, don't be bloody ridiculous,' she turned round and said. Then she went back to her book.

'Right then.' I doodled around and she looked up again.

'You must be missing a brain cell somewhere,' she went. 'The sense cell.'

'All right Marigold no problem girl, only thought I'd mention it like us being so cosy and that.'

'Nicky, maybe you don't remember, but you've got a good loving woman, am I right?'

'One of the best I'm telling you. Correction. The best. Noreen, quality woman.'

'And what do you think she'd say?'

'Don't have to know innit? You ain't going to tell her. I aren't going to tell her. No problem Marigold I ain't grieved, all sorted mate you don't want to do it, your privilege. Some other time eh?'

She put her book down again a bit and she cackled.

'I have to say, Nicky,' she went. 'You never stop. Eleven years old you were just the same. A hundred and eleven you'll be just the same. Chancer, that's what you are. See it, go for it.'

'Only reckoned I'd mention it Marigold,' I went. 'See how the land lies and that.'

'Yes, well, it lies very bumpy round here.'

'Fair enough.'

We went back to our bevies and our books. She laughed again I grant her that. No problem.

She was a class A bird that Marigold.

CHAPTER TWENTY- SEVEN

THEY LAID SIEGE to Walthamstow.

I got off the 48 at Baker's Arms and thought about stepping in the save-the-world shop for a bite. Unfortunately there was a blockage on Hoe St. They overturned a bus and burned it.

How you overturned a bus anyhow was one skill they never taught on their knock-you-off-the-dole-and-pretend-it's-training course. In Pakistan they only got single deckers so it was never one of their transferable skills neither. Double decker, wheels up and burning very nice for keeping your mitts warm.

In the bargain it was hard to reckon how they got their payback on us by burning up some bus. Only conclusion I drew was they got a bit of a downer on Walthamstow in general.

When I stepped off that 48 there was never one single geezer or bird on the street.

Shops got their shutters down. Locked up like the next ice age. I ran along Lea Bridge and up the one way back to Hoe St keeping flat by the buildings. I peeked round the corner. I fucking soon peeked off again. Shot whistled over my bonce.

Maybe not aimed my way seeing as ten other shots were whistling other places. All the same a wise geezer kept his titfer on.

I belled Rameez.

When he answered it sounded worse his end. Fucking great boom like the world just ended on the High St.

Rameez still cool. 'They got mortars,' he goes casual like they got samosas.

'Mortars,' I goes. Mortars I clocked in Pakistan. What I wondered was them getting their mortars past customs up Dover when I got problems getting a few cases of ciggies in.

''Scuse me Nicky,' he goes. 'I just got to get under the counter here.' Bit of a pause. Boom. 'Now carry on my bro.'

'The fuck you are Rameez?'

'Sports shop. Only came in for some baseball bats. We got to get extra help and they not all kitted out.'

'Old Bill present?'

'I think Nicky it maybe came to their attention by now.'

'What you doing next Rameez or what?'

'I getting the fuck out of here Nicky and waste a few, the fuck you reckon?'

'Clock you soon eh?'

'Soon. Post office.'

'Got you.'

Jimmy Foley was on my line.

'All right Jimmy?' I goes.

'Nicky I never met anything like this Nicky this is fuckin' fuckin' fuckin' wild they only just blew out Poundstretcher and the health shop Nicky—'

'Jimmy!' I gets in.

'—you never heard Nicky bangs whooshes—'

'Jimmy!'

'Yes Nicky?'

'Shut the fuck up. Everybody you find. Post office.'

'Yes Nicky.'

I ran round the back by the Windmill over Orford Rd over the bridge and on St Mary Rd. Few people now all running like fuck the other way.

And bangs and whooshes and whoomphs and crashes. War zone.

Sounded like they got two parties. One party coming up Hoe St from Baker's Arms, other party coming down Hoe St from The Bell. Shots from both and mortars landing on the High St. They were invading.

I belled TT.

'Official agencies are mobilising every resource,' he went straight off for the bosses or the papers.

'TT!' I went.

'Yes!' he went.

'It's me,' I went.

'Fuck's bloody sake,' he goes not so official. 'You something to do with this Nicky you fucking little bastard?'

'Fuck you think?' I goes. 'You still planning negotiations with these geezers or what? Get your fucking bonzos by the post office TT. Ten four.' I was gone.

Jamil's boys were getting closer. Crouching down St Mary Rd I ran forward. Lay down by the steps for the pedestrian crossing.

Blast came off the Central. They hit the station in front of a train just pulling away. Crash of brakes.

I backed off and down Stainforth Rd up Church Hill. One motor coming down. Seemed like it never heard about any problems. Old biddie about eighty quite happy. Got a disabled sticker park anywhere. Maybe have a spot of trouble getting her pension out the post office just now. I let her go on. No sense worrying her.

By the post office the boys gathering.

I ran over Hoe St keeping my bonce down and joined them.

Rameez and his posse about twenty. Then Jimmy Foley Dean Longmore Wayne Sapsford Sherry McAllister Elvis Littlejohn Mercedes Marty Fisherman Ricky Hurlock Shelley Rosario Paulette James Chantel Livingstone Tina Duffy and a lot. Ronnie Good hard man. Word went round quick. They all heard Ilford was coming for Walthamstow.

Then Old Bill arrived. Too soon for the armoury to get there so they got plods. PCs Karen Mohammed and the bird got big tits Burns. All the pigs out the office on the market and coming off Greenleaf Rd. CID ready for clues who the villains were, TT and DS O'Malley out of Chingford already. George Marshall my warrant officer now a civilian. Andy my probation officer lurking, maybe do a spot of counselling somewhere. They were coming in.

Only they all stood there waiting for a leader.

'Barricades!' yelled Ronnie Good.

'No barricades!' went TT. 'The police service will arrest these people.'

Another explosion went off by the precinct. Took out a couple of pensioners.

'You wanna arrest that?' goes Ronnie.

Ronnie Good dealt in smarties and whizz and never needed any extra muscle. Ronnie said barricades you got barricades.

We dragged the market stalls over. Tables out of Pizza Hut. Stacks of books out of Hammicks. Typing paper out of Rymans. Then sacks of rice and lentils and piles of yam off the groceries. Near on a hundred people carrying, took minutes Ronnie leading. Last off we got the vans belonged to market traders.

Formed a big semi-circle guarding the end of the High St and both ways up Hoe St.

Then they were here.

Past the cinema one party following the walls, crouching down firing rifles on anything moved. Down the middle the street they got two Securicor vans they probably hijacked by the courts collecting prisoners. I hoped they did some damage. Other way off Baker's Arms they got to come over the bridge by the Central or down on the track and up again. Bridge made a target so they went down.

Imtiaz was the only one on our side got a shooter. He was busy. I lay down low.

TT beside me started taking a peek over our sacks of rice. I hauled on his plates and yanked him back down. 'Fuckin' hell TT,' I went. 'I hate to save fuckin' Old Bill only you know these geezers shoot you soon as take a shit or what? They for real man.'

'Fuck,' he goes.

'You getting the bleeding army in or what?'

Then a chopper arrived. Went down to park by the bus station.

'More like it,' I went.

Only it turned out it was the fucking TV.

They all got out the chopper and then there was serious noise. Jamil's boys came out the Central and shot a couple. Not very media friendly.

'We got to attack,' went Rameez. 'Sitting fucking ducks.'

He and his boys making petrol bombs fast as they got the petrol out the vans.

'Go!' he yelled.

Dozen of his boys leaped out round the library and up the Kurdish supermarket and by the cinema. Two got hit. All threw their bombs. No flies on them, got to be short on practice only they all went off. Whoomph.

Then armed Old Bill came up the market. Four of them, all they got in the area. Helmets. Big vests. They started firing across the bus station.

'All right Nicky?' goes Rameez.

'Shitting myself now you mention it.'

'I meaning you all right for attack?'

'Oh sure any time. After you.'

'For Walthamstow!'

'Yeah!'

I stayed down.

Then they were on us.

Hundreds it seemed like. Half out of Pakistan half Ilford by the look. When they came in close they took one last shooting before it was hand jobs.

Jimmy Foley went down.

'Fuck!' he screamed. 'Fucking fuck they got me!'

'Where Jimmy?'

'Fuckin' hell!' he yelled out.

'Cool it Jimmy,' I went. 'Wake the bleeding baby. Where they got you?'

'Nicky I got shot for you again you fucker! In the fuckin' shoulder!'

'That all? Christ Jimmy you got another one no problem. Think of them bleeding birds come round again clock your exit wounds geezer.'

They came over the top. They pulled out their clubs and blades. Half of them got long long knives I never fancied a stabbing off.

One of them climbing over our barricade I hit him so hard with a bat it snapped his kneecap. Rameez shafted one with his sword. Imtiaz shot one. Aftab and Afzal close together whacking like clockwork. On that barricade it was thirty of us and ten of them. They fell back.

Then up the market came Mickey Cousins and Tweedle-dum and Tweedledummer and a dozen. Mickey lost his reason. Never show his mug this way. Not professional he got angry.

They came again on all sides.

It was mad.

Dean Longmore got one in the side. Gulzar went down screaming. Rameez got gravy pouring off his bonce. It was hand to hand whacking and stabbing. Noise was something awful.

I clocked Paulette punch for punch with some geezer in a scarf. Big bird Paulette. He went down. Tina Duffy who I put it up years back, she got a dagger sticking out her arm, crying and wailing. PC Burns both tits in action swinging and swatting. DS O'Malley went down. They were flooding over. I stood back to back with Rameez then I felt him crumble. Next I got a fucking almighty crack where he was stood before. I went down. Fucking collar bone. Again. I yelled out. It was left one as it goes, fortunate.

Rameez was bleeding by me.

'You all right mate?' I goes.

'Been better Nicky. Got a stick in the neck.'

'You hold on mate.'

One of Ilfords was following up on Rameez. Same geezer smacked me probably. When he jumped down over the barrier I grabbed Rameez's sword lying there and stuck it straight up his hooter. Made the most horrible mess I ever clocked in my life. Took him so hard it nearly cracked my good collar bone in the bargain.

Old Bill arrived in numbers. Late as ever and never equipped. Spot of CS gas fucking pathetic. But they got in behind the barricades and got their uniforms dirty. We got the numbers now. Old Bill never even knew which side was which only I never cared they arrested the fucking lot of us, nice quiet cell a lot better than this.

Then Bridget Tansley appeared beside me with a mike.

'Bridget?' I turned round and said. Bridget off the *Walthamstow Guardian*. She was talking direct to camera.

'IT IS HELL ON HOE ST!' she shouted.

Fuck we were live on air.

'NO ONE KNOWS WHAT IS HAPPENING. THIS IS WAR. WALTHAMSTOW IS BEING INVADED. IT IS HELL ON HOE ST.'

'Fuck's sake Bridget,' I goes. 'This ain't doing me no favours with Noreen's mum and dad me fighting on the news.'

'Two of your television team have been wounded including your reporter,' she was yelling on. So she took over the spot. 'Mayhem has broken out. Beside me is local character Nicky Burkett. Nicky what are your comments on the current situation?'

'Fucking fucking fuck!' Some fucker just hit my collar bone.

'And here coming towards us is another well-known local character and car dealer Mickey Cousins.'

Wayne and Aftab and Elvis and Shelley all went on Mickey. His boys got separated thirty seconds. He went down and they gave him a kicking for afters.

Then when he was only thinking on climbing up again he got another intervention. This time it was TT.

DS Holdsworth out of Chingford, live on the evening news, went over to the injured man. Just when car dealer Mickey Cousins was staggering to his knees DS Holdsworth kicked him so hard in the kidneys, twice, that it seemed he was trying to give him a transplant there and then. Mr Cousins went down again.

All those years of graft then TT blew all his promotions live on the early evening. Fucking amusing I got to cackle.

Jamil's boys were retreating. Old Bill there in spades now.

'I think the tide has turned now,' Bridget was shouting. Then she got shot. Took the mike and her hand with it. Only a scratch but she started screaming, never been shot before.

I staggered back and clocked Rameez sat leaning beside a wall. Leaning in the air not on the wall. He still got a sticker coming out his neck. Seemed like it missed the business area only he was never touching it. I slid down by him. He was wheezing.

Then I got a nightmare.

Over across the square one bloody geezer was crawling at me. Wounded fair all over. Stabbed and maybe sliced. He was never a happy geezer and it looked like he was blaming me for his whole predicament.

Jamil Khan Jamal.

He was bent on serious mischief.

No one looked like they took notice. He picked up a sticker off the floor already covered in blood. He made his advance.

'No,' I goes.

'All yours Nicky,' wheezes Rameez.

'You little fucker,' goes Jamil. It got to be he heard me described by Mickey Cousins. 'You little fucker,' he went again, fond of the expression.

I remembered how I was supposed to kill Jamil or old Abdul came round killing me. Tell the truth I never was keen though.

'No,' I goes again.

He lifted himself up and he held that sticker high and he was making for me and it looked like I was down for relegation.

I whipped the blade out of Rameez's neck beside me.

Just then someone grabbed Jamil's hand from behind. Only his body kept coming while his hand was pulled right back. His body collapsed all over me.

194

Only in between us was that blade out of Rameez's neck and it was pointing upwards.

Slap in the gut no messing.

He yelled out curdling. That blade was in deep.

'Oh no not again!' went Noreen. It was Noreen caught his mitt back. It was Noreen turned up in time to save my breathing.

'Oh no not again!' she went case I never heard her the first time. 'You never killed some geezer all over again Nicky!'

'Too early to tell Noreen,' I goes. Jamil slobbering and bleeding all over me, still alive so far only I never took any bets. 'Too early to tell, maybe he makes it maybe he never. Anyhow look who's the aggressor here, self-defence in a court of law am I right?'

'But he might be dying!'

'Fuckin' hope so.'

'Oh Nicky!'

'Noreen I loves you!'

'Oh Nicky!'

'Fuck's sake Nicky,' goes Rameez wheezing. 'You find me a fucking medic or what? Only that blade holding me together and you got to borrow it away.'

'Sorry Rameez mate. Patch you up soon as I can get out from under. Feel a bit weak be honest. Get you up Casualty though I reckon soon as them paras get here.'

He was wheezing for definite.

'Bridget!' I goes.

'Nicky is that you under there?'

'You all right Bridget?'

'Yes. Yes I think so.'

'That chopper there get us all up Whipps Cross?'

No point waiting for the ambulance chopper, be sat waiting half the night on account of the cuts. TV chopper fit the bill right well.

She was gone. Moments she was back with the TV crew round us. They lifted Rameez up nice and gentle and took him by them.

They helped me up for joining him in Casualty and for getting out the area before anyone found my fist still in Jamil's gut.

They took Bridget for her wound and for the story. They took Noreen for keeping me company.

We got in that chopper and believe it we pulled away in that sky.

I looked back down and I clocked Walthamstow lying wasted under us. Made me romantic and sad.

'Noreen I reckon I loves you,' I went again.

'Oh Nicky. Such a pity you killed another one down there.'

'No telling who stuck Jamil Noreen. No weapon ever found.' I got it in my pocket. 'And he never croaked yet anyhow. Maybe get him next time.'

'Oh Nicky.'

No winning with women. No point asking who started the whole fucking business. Instead we got a little cuddle up. Reckoned I could win her round with a spot of loving and maybe a spell in hospital.

That chopper rose over the Central and went down Hoe St and turned left on Lea Bridge Rd and a few seconds we were at Whipps Cross.

Bit later that Casualty got very busy down Whipps Cross. We got there before the rush though. By the time they brought in hundreds bleeding and howling we were tucked up nice and warm in our hospital beds and sipping our tea and clocking their nurses.

Don't miss the other titles
in the NICKY BURKETT series

'*Ingenious, his street talk sizzles with wit and invention.*' **Literary Review**

'*Like a hybrid of Only Fools and Horses and a hyperviolent Tarantino.*' **The Big Issue**

'*More street cred than wheel clamps.*'
Daily Telegraph

'*A wonderful thriller. An absolute cracker!*'
The Independent

'*The pleasure is intense… an unmatched ear for the shady melodies of London's street.*'
Time Out

'*A consistently funny and entertaining book.*' **The Times**

'*Funny and entertaining*' **The Times**

'*Unputdownable*' **Big Issue**

'*Engaging, eventful and original*' **Literary Review**

'*Sleazy, violent and laugh out loud funny*'
Amazon reviewer

'*Audacious and outrageous.*' **Daily Telegraph**

'*Jaunty, exhilarating and original, with a feeling for street life that renders it sexy and poignant.*' **Literary Review**

'*A fast, funny trawl through the territory of London's new outlaw underclass. It is a masterly piece of storytelling.*'
Financial Times

'*A short, sharp, shock of a novel.*' **GQ**

'*Funny, violent and vivid.*' **Sunday Times**